Mark Cooke was born in 1961 in Manchester where he grew up. Since leaving school he has worked in a variety of jobs and recently gained a degree in English at Lancaster University.

This is his first novel.

AN ENGLISH
SUPERHERO

Mark Cooke

An
English Superhero

Nightingale Books

A CIP catalogue record for this title is
available from the British Library
ISBN 1 903491 11 8

*Nightingale Books is an imprint of
Pegasus Elliot MacKenzie Publishers Ltd.*
www.pegasuspublishers.com

First Published in 2002

**Nightingale Books
Sheraton House Castle Park
Cambridge England**

Printed & Bound in Great Britain

Dedication

For my mother, a very special person

CHAPTER ONE

WITCHES WOODS

Have you ever wondered why all the Superheroes are American? Well, you're not the only one. What is it with America? Is there something in their water? Is there something in their coffee? Who can say? Well, I'm here to tell you not all Superheroes are American. And this is the story of an English Superhero. His name is Bobby Coleman.

There were one or two differences between Bobby and your average American Superhero. He didn't wear a brightly coloured costume for a start. He didn't boast to be faster than a speeding bullet. He wasn't from another planet, and he *certainly* didn't wear his underpants on the outside of his trousers. The most surprising difference of all though, is his age. For Bobby is only twelve years old.

How did the youngster become a Superhero? Well, it all took place one Christmas Day not so long ago. Bobby had been given a budgie by his parents, which he immediately called Arnie, and he decided to take his new friend for a walk to show him some of the local sights.

Everything was fine and dandy until Arnie discovered he could fly, and as soon as he had made this startling discovery he flew over the trees and into the local woods to find other budgies.

Bobby shot after his budgie and clambered over the red iron gates that were designed to keep children out of the woods and jumped into the long grass on the other side.

But Arnie was gone. One hundred percent gone. And finding a budgie in these woods was like finding a needle in a haystack.

Bobby soon realised *he* was lost as well. So he had lost himself and his budgie all in the space of ten minutes. And this was not good. It would be dark shortly and he was lost, and he was lost in Witches Woods.

Local legend said that in the dark ages witches would come to the woods and perform all manner of witchcraft. Perhaps they turned local children into hamsters, or created magic potions that made short people tall. Or perhaps they just met up for a good old gossip. Nobody was really sure what they did, but the local villagers of the time burnt all the witches they could find, so they couldn't have been *too* impressed with what they were doing. Although that was many moons ago.

Nowadays, all the local children would sneak into the woods during the day and run around without any fear at all. Would they play in the woods after it had gone dark? They would rather hammer nails into wood with their heads and young Bobby Coleman was about to find out why.

Night dropped very fast in Milltown.

Plonk!

Bobby was still able to see quite well as there was a full moon tonight. Was he going in the right direction though? Who knows? He *certainly* didn't. Maybe he should sit down and wait until morning, but it was far too cold to stay still and he didn't fancy spending all night in Witches Woods.

Witches Woods, what a name. It wouldn't be so bad if he had got lost in Fluffy Woods, or Lovely Woods, but he had to go and get himself lost in deep, dark Witches Woods.

12

"It's lucky I don't believe in witches," he muttered quietly as he stumbled deeper into the woods.

After a while Bobby realised that, rather than getting darker, it was gradually becoming lighter. Then he saw the lights. Strange green lights. He knew it was a bad idea to go towards them, but he did so anyway, because he was a nosey so-and-so. Maybe it was the moonlight shining on the pond, he fooled himself into believing, as the light became brighter and brighter.

It wasn't long before he found himself in a small clearing in the woods and right in front of him there was a fire burning. Although *this* was no ordinary fire because the light it gave out was green and it didn't seem to be giving off any heat. He crouched down by the fire and held his hands above the flames. "Just what I need on a freezing cold December night," he said with a wry smile. "A fire without heat."

As Bobby crouched there wondering what kind of fire this was, he heard sounds coming from behind him, and as he swung around to see who was making this noise, he lost his balance and fell into the fire. But the flames did not burn. He quickly lifted himself from the fire and listened intently. There was definitely something coming through the trees towards him, and it was bigger than anything wild that lived in *these* woods. Who would be out here after dark? The noises were very close now. He wanted to run but his legs wouldn't respond. He stood there transfixed.

A dark shape floated out of the trees and drifted through the cold night air. It came to rest right before him. The dark shape spoke. "Well, well, what have we here?"

Bobby felt ice running through his veins. He was too terrified to speak, and even if he did find his voice, what was he going to say to a witch?

"Has the cat got your tongue?" asked the witch.

Bobby was too scared to answer.

The witch spoke again. "I *said*, has the cat got your tongue?"

Bobby didn't know what had got his tongue and now his knees had begun to knock together.

"Well then, my silent friend, what brings you to Witches Woods at this late hour? Don't you know that dark and dangerous things happen out here at night?"

Okay, it's dark, I'm lost, I'm listening to a witch, and perhaps, with any luck, I'm dreaming all this.

"You are not dreaming," said the witch, interrupting his thoughts. "This is *really* happening. Have you *nothing* to say for yourself?"

"Please don't turn me into a newt!" Bobby blurted out.

The witch let out a high pitched cackle. "So you do have a tongue in your head, after all. Don't worry, I've not turned anyone into a newt in centuries, and only then because I was very, very annoyed. And you haven't annoyed me... *yet*."

"Are you a witch?" asked Bobby.

The witch hunched up her shoulders. "This *is* Witches Woods. What did you expect to find in a wood with that name? Crocodiles!" The witch began cackling again.

Blimey, she's got a hell of a sense of humour.

"You *need* a good sense of humour when you're a witch."

"How did you know what I was thinking?" gulped Bobby.

"Because I'm a witch, numbskull. We wouldn't be half as scary if we were the same as everybody else." The witch said her name was Thelma and she was over three hundred years old. She told him that even though witches scared the pants off people most of them were really quite

14

harmless. She said three witches used the woods and they were quite happy to pull a few crafty stunts now and again to frighten off the locals. Then they could get on with casting their spells and mixing their potions without being disturbed. Every night they ensured these woods were a *very* frightening place to be in after dark.

"How do you manage that?" asked Bobby.

"Magic!" cried the witch.

"What kind of magic?"

"Well, as it goes dark each night we put a spell on the woods. This spell gives people the jitters. It makes them see things that aren't there. It makes them hear strange ghostly voices, and it generally spooks the life out of them. It's worked that way for hundreds of years, and it's the smoke from the fire that casts the spell on the woods."

Bobby gazed at the green flames. "It's a magic fire then. I wondered why I didn't get burnt when I fell in the flames."

"You fell in the flames?"

"Yes."

"Then your life is going to be very different from now on."

"In what way?"

"You will soon see."

Bobby said it would be nice if Thelma could use a touch of her magic to get him out of the woods, because his parents would begin worrying about him soon, and he didn't want to miss Christmas dinner, especially the Xmas pudding, and he was getting a bit chilly and wanted a hot bath.

Thelma pointed in a northerly direction and told Bobby he was two minutes from the red iron gates.

Two minutes, I must have been going round in circles.

"I think you must have been," agreed the witch,

reading his thoughts again.

I wish she would stop doing that.

"I can't help it," said Thelma, butting in again. "You have very clear thoughts, but you also have the sense of direction of a cross-eyed bat."

Bobby ignored the insult. "Do you have to read all my thoughts? It's very disturbing. What if I thought something that wasn't very nice, about you?"

"Then I would turn you into a gerbil."

"Er, then it's lucky for me that I think you are without doubt the most lovely and beautiful witch I have ever met," Bobby said with a cheeky smile.

The witch stroked her long black hair. "Yes, I am, aren't I? Which is lucky for you, because gerbils don't get much Xmas pudding."

Bobby waved goodbye and began walking back to the red iron gates. After a couple of steps he stopped and turned round. "By the way, you haven't seen any wayward budgies around here have you? Mine seems to have done a runner, I mean a flyer."

The witch shook her head. "No, I haven't seen your budgie," and then her eyes sparkled like tiny green jewels. "I could magic one up for you if you like. Witch Rule Number 34 says I shouldn't really do this, but seeing as it's Christmas..."

"That would be great," Bobby enthused. "I've never had a present off a witch before. If you don't count my Aunty Ethel."

There was a supernatural gleam in Thelma's eye and she coughed a little for dramatic effect:

"Cats are cats as well we know,
And bats are bats or so we're told,
Birds are birds or so it's said,

16

So perch a budgie on his head."

As the witch pointed a crooked finger at Bobby there was a tiny clap of thunder, a bright green flash of light and, all of a sudden, there was a little green budgie sitting on his head.

The budgie fluttered down onto his shoulder and the young boy turned his head slightly and admired the little fellow. The youngster was suitably impressed with this, until he noticed there was something different about this budgie. He smiled a little awkwardly. "That was very good, Thelma, but this budgie is green."

"So what?"

"Arnie was blue."

"Oops!" cried Thelma. "I'm sorry, I'm a bit rusty on the old budgie magic, and you didn't tell me what colour your budgie was. I'm sure nobody will notice."

"Perhaps not," said Bobby. "Anyway, thanks for all your help, and thanks for not turning me into a gerbil. I'll never think of witches as warty old hags on broomsticks again."

"Oh, we still use broomsticks," remarked the witch with a crafty grin.

"What for? Flying around on."

"No silly, for sweeping out our cottages."

Bobby laughed. "Haven't you heard of hoovers?"

"Of course we have," cackled the witch. "I could magic the cottage clean if I really wanted to, but some things are best done the old fashioned way. Well, it's getting late young man and I think you should be on your way. Come and visit me sometime, I'm in these woods every Tuesday and Thursday nights." The witch paused and gave him a wary glare. "Now you have been bathed in the magic flames you may find there will be one or two changes in your life."

"I can handle one or two changes," said Bobby with true bravado.

"We will see."

The young boy stared at the little green budgie sitting on his shoulder. "Do you think I should change Arnie's name, seeing he's a different budgie?"

"Our little friend likes that name," Thelma replied.

"How do you know that?"

"Budgies have thoughts as well," chortled the witch.

Bobby patted his little budgie on the head. "Come on then, Arnie, it's home time." He looked up to say goodbye, but Thelma had disappeared. "I suppose I should have seen that coming. Witches certainly have a flair for the dramatic."

He climbed back over the red iron gates and dropped back onto the avenue that led away from the woods. He wound his way home, with his new budgie perched on his shoulder, like some pirate and his parrot.

He was trying to come to terms with what had just happened, but he was only twelve years old, and thinking too deeply at that tender age can sometimes makes your brain turn hot. He shrugged his shoulders. There are bound to be witches in the world considering there are so many books and films about them. It was only a matter of time before he bumped into one, especially in a place called Witches Woods.

Bobby wandered in through the front door to be greeted by Sparky the dog bouncing all over him. He went into the dining room where his mum, dad and younger sister Anna were tucking into their Christmas dinner.

Mr Coleman looked up with his mouth crammed full of turkey and said in a muffled voice. "Mmmppfff mnnfff snnnf mmpp."

"Sorry dad, I didn't quite catch that."

Mrs Coleman peered at him over her gold rimmed glasses and translated her husband's words. "He said we started Christmas dinner without you because you've been so long walking that budgie."

"Oh right," said Bobby. "I thought he said, Mmmppfff mnnfff snnnf mmpp."

Mr Coleman swallowed his mouthful of turkey. "Don't try to be clever, son. You've got to *be* clever before you can start acting that way."

As Bobby didn't understand what his dad was prattling on about, he sat down and tucked into his Christmas dinner.

Mr Coleman gawped across the table. "Since when does anyone take a budgie for a walk, lame brain?"

"What's wrong with taking a budgie for a walk?"

"Nothing, if you've got a lame brain," sneered Mr Coleman. "I suppose you'll take Sparky out flying later on." He found this so amusing he nearly choked on some turkey.

"Could we *please* eat just *one* meal in this house in peace and quiet," interrupted Mrs Coleman in an exasperated voice.

"It's not *me*," protested Bobby. "It's blabber mouth over there."

"If the *pair* of you don't pipe down the telly's staying off all night."

Bobby and his dad immediately buttoned it, as they both knew they couldn't survive all night without the telly.

After the turkey it was cracker pulling time. The four members of the Coleman family sat around the table pulling crackers, wearing silly hats, telling terrible cracker jokes and discovering what pathetic toys their crackers contained.

Bobby got a tiny plastic magnifying glass out of his cracker. "That will come in handy," he muttered as he threw it in the bin.

Mrs Coleman was reading out her cracker joke as Bobby got up to leave the room. "What is black and white and red all over?"

"How about a black and white red thing?" said Bobby. He knew it wasn't the right answer, but it couldn't be much worse than the proper joke. As he climbed the stairs to his room he began to feel dizzy and needed to lie down for a while.

As he was lying quietly on his bed, his little sister came into his room and sprang up next to him.

"Why is the budgie green?" she asked.

"Is this one of those stupid cracker jokes?"

"No, Bobby. Why is *your* budgie green?"

"It's got to be some colour, Anna."

"But it was blue when you left the house."

Trust the youngest person in the house to notice that. If he had come back with a six foot budgie riding a motorbike his parents wouldn't have noticed, but there's no fooling a six year old.

"It's a magic budgie, Anna," he whispered, putting a single finger up to his lips, "but you're not to tell a soul."

"I won't," chirruped Anna. "It will be our secret." Then she gazed into his eyes. "Why are your eyes green?"

"Don't be silly, Anna, my eyes are brown."

"Not any more they're not," giggled the little girl.

Bobby went to the mirror in his bedroom and sure enough his eyes were green instead of brown.

"They look nice, Bobby," said Anna. "They make you look like a cat."

Suddenly there was a loud shout from downstairs.

"Bobby, Anna, The Wizard of Oz is coming on!"

The children jumped off the bed and dashed downstairs.

For Christmas wouldn't be Christmas without The Wizard of Oz on the telly.

CHAPTER TWO

CHANGES

Boxing Day.

Bobby woke up, jumped out of bed, and went over to his mirror. His eyes were still green. "Brown eyes, green eyes, what's the difference?" he said to his reflection.

He went downstairs and found a note on the sideboard. He picked it up and read it:

Gone to Uncle Donalds. Back for tea. If you're hungry, there's turkey in the fridge. Love mum.

Arnie flew over and landed on his shoulder.

"How did you get out of your cage?"

You left the cage door open.

Bobby glanced around the room. "Who said that?" He stared at his budgie. Surely not. But maybe this is a magic budgie. It did appear out of thin air after all.

"Did you say something?" Bobby asked, not expecting any answer.

I can't speak.

"How can you speak without moving your beak?"

I just told you I can't speak.

Bobby seemed puzzled by this. Then a tiny light bulb lit over his head as he realised what was going on. "I think I get it, I can read your thoughts, can't I?"

Wow. Well done, Einstein. Give the boy a round of applause.

"Are all budgies as rude as you?"

How would I know? I didn't even know I was a budgie until you told me. What exactly is a budgie?

Bobby walked over to the mirror and pointed to the little green budgie sat on his shoulder. "That's a budgie."

I'm very pretty, aren't I?

Arnie preened a couple of his feathers.

I'm very hungry, too. Got any sesame seeds?

"We've got loads of stuff. It is Christmas, you know."

Is it?

Bobby opened the fridge and peered inside. He took out the plate with the big turkey on it. "Fancy a slice of turkey, Arnie?"

I think that would be cannibalism, don't you?

"Oh yes, sorry," he said sheepishly. "I've got a packet full of millet over there."

That will do very nicely.

As he went to put the turkey back in the fridge, the plate slipped out of his hands. "Oh no!" he yelled, as it tumbled to the floor.

Arnie glided off his shoulder.

As the plate was about to hit the floor and smash into a thousand pieces, something very unusual happened. The plate stopped in mid-fall, about ten centimetres from the floor and just hung there. What was going on? He swivelled round to speak to Arnie, but the budgie was frozen in mid-flight. Very strange. The kitchen clock had also stopped ticking. It seemed as if time had stopped. He bent down and plucked the plate from its mid-air position and stood up again.

As he put the turkey back in the fridge the clock began to tick again and the budgie resumed his flight.

Bobby scratched his head. "Did you just see what happened?"

No, but I see you caught the plate before it hit the

23

ground. Well done, sir.

"I didn't stop the plate hitting the ground. It stopped itself. Watch this." Bobby dropped the plate again and shouted. "Oh no!"

And the plate fell to the ground and smashed into a thousand pieces.

Arnie nodded his head slowly.

That's very impressive.

"*That* didn't happen before," said the astounded boy.

You don't say. It'll be fun watching you explain this one to your mum and dad.

Mr and Mrs Coleman arrived home to a ruined turkey, and after they had finished bouncing up and down, and ranting and raving, they sent Bobby to get a Chinese takeaway. Mr Coleman was secretly pleased as this meant he wouldn't be taking turkey sandwiches to work in his lunchbox for weeks and weeks and weeks.

After Bobby had eaten his sweet and sour chicken he went upstairs and thought about his new powers. He wasn't in the same league as the American Superheroes. He didn't have any Superstrength. He wasn't incredibly fast. He couldn't fly or climb up the side of buildings. But having any kind of Superpower was better than having none at all. Although he didn't admit it, he was a little disappointed.

Later on that day Bobby discovered another Superpower.

He was exploring Milltown's old haunted railway station with Katy Fenton, also known as Kat. The brave and sneaky pair crept up into the top control room where the mad ghost of the old station master was supposed to haunt.

Local history said the ghost was mad because he'd been run over by a train his brother had been driving, and,

I suppose, that would make anyone mad.

As the youngsters crept through all the old rooms, the dust was making Bobby's eyes water, and he gave them a good old rub with the palms of his hands to help clear his vision.

Kat was feeling rather spooked by the ghostly surroundings. Then, to her great surprise, she realised her friend had vanished. "Where are you, Bobby?" she asked in a timid voice.

Now Bobby didn't know what she meant as he was standing right next to her. "I'm right here."

Kat let out a terrified scream and ran out of the room shrieking. "Run! Bobby, run! I've heard the mad ghost speak!" She leapt down the stairs in one go and crashed out of the old railway station.

Bobby had no idea why she had done this. He hadn't heard anyone speak. As he was wondering about this he squinted into an old dusty mirror on the wall, but he wasn't in the reflection. "Blimey, I'm invisible," he whispered. "No wonder Kat was hearing voices. I must have frightened the life out of her." Which was quite funny really.

Bobby didn't know how, or why, he'd disappeared, but this was obviously another Superpower and a rather exciting one as well.

The invisible boy left the haunted railway station and went into the village. He was wandering around the shops when he noticed his mother in the shoe shop looking at some trainers. He walked into the shop and stood next to his mum and heard her say to the shop assistant. "I can't decide whether my son will like these trainers."

"You must be joking," said the invisible boy. "I wouldn't be seen dead in them." Then he walked back out of the shop leaving his mum and the shop assistant looking extremely pale and shocked.

As he was wondering what to do next, he saw his reflection in the butcher's window. "Hello, I'm back again."

CHAPTER THREE

UNDERGROUND

Bobby was out on New Year's Eve with his best friends, Katy Fenton and Micky Jordan.

Katy was called Kat for obvious reasons, and Micky was called Teabag because he was round and wet. All children have nicknames. It is one of their laws. Bobby Coleman's nickname was Coleslaw, but as this was a pretty weak nickname everyone stuck with Bobby.

As it was snowing, the three children had each brought out a big kitchen tray so they could go tobogganing down the nearby cycle path. Their parents would not have approved, as they thought the cycle path was a dangerous place to play. But the twelve year olds knew better.

For a start, now it was snowing, the cycle path was too slippy for cyclists to use and, anyhow, the last time a cyclist had actually used this cycle path was two and a half years ago, and so the children felt it was as safe as houses.

They began whizzing down the steep path at various speeds, bumping into trees and countless other objects. It was all good fun until Kat crazily decided it would be a good idea to do a triple decker slide. The three daredevils squeezed onto one tray at the top of the cycle path and pushed themselves off.

All the birds in the neighbourhood were landing in nearby trees to get a good ringside view. This was going to be the most exciting thing to happen on the cycle path since a local school teacher fell off her bike and slightly grazed her knee about five years ago. This is what you call real entertainment.

The tray quickly gathered momentum and soon it was travelling at a breathtaking speed.

All the birds were holding their breath in suspense as the children went shooting down the hill, screaming all the way.

Then disaster struck. The tray hit a patch of black ice, as the speed merchants reached maximum velocity, and they suddenly became airborne. The three tray travellers left the ground and shot over a hedge at an incredible speed.

The birds put their wings and feathers over their eyes and ears, as the tray flew towards a nearby pond.

Luckily, for our flying threesome, the pond was frozen, and they shot across the ice on their backsides and disappeared into a bank of snow on the other side. Thunk! Thunk! Thunk!

The gathered birds whistled and applauded as they hadn't been entertained this much for years. Then they flew off home as it was getting dark and nothing the children did now could follow that.

The three children were deep inside the snowbank and they seemed to be balanced on the edge of a very steep slope. They teetered this way and they teetered that way and then they fell over and over and down and down, and just as it seemed they would never stop they suddenly slid to a halt. All daylight had gone and they were deep underground. An eerie grey light lit up wherever it was they were and everywhere smelt damp and musty.

"Well, that was a buzz," said Kat, wiping some of the mud off her clothes.

Teabag picked a few twigs out of his hair. "Where are we?"

Bobby squinted around the dank dark cave. "I don't think we're in Milltown any more."

"What makes you say that, Bobby?" Kat said sarcastically. "Would it be the absence of houses, or people, or animals? Or maybe it's because we're ten miles underground in a dark grey cave with water trickling down the walls?"

Bobby looked a little wounded. "There's no need to jump down my throat. I was only making an observation."

"Perhaps, when you two have stopped bickering," whispered a worried Teabag, "we might start looking for a way out."

The three children wandered through the chilly grey corridors of wherever it was they were, but it was no good, they were very lost indeed.

As they searched the caverns Bobby's mind was wandering. I'm beginning to make a habit of this. I wonder where else I can get myself lost, because I'm getting rather good at it. Why can't I be more like Spiderman or Superman? They'd be out of here in a flash.

The children were cold and hungry and their spirits were low and then, without warning, everything took a turn for the worse.

Whoosh!

They were swept up in a large net. They hung suspended from the cave ceiling gently swinging from side to side.

Kat shrugged. "It's just not our day, is it?"

"You're right, Bobby," confirmed Teabag. "We're not in Milltown anymore."

And then a loud whooping alarm began to sound.

Kat was deeply worried about this large net and the

wailing alarm. "Who would set a trap like this?"

Bobby stuck his fingers in his ears. "I think we'll be finding out pretty soon."

Teabag cupped his hands to his mouth and yelled. "Has anyone got a pen knife?"

Nobody had a pen knife.

The alarm ceased wailing.

Bobby was pleased that Teabag was thinking of escape and not just swinging there accepting what had happened. He realised he'd been very childish about his new Superpowers and he should be grateful for them and buck up and start acting like a real Superhero. From now on you would see a very different Bobby Coleman. He wondered how his Superpowers could get them out of this mess. What if he could freeze time again? That might give him enough breathing space to think of an escape. He took a deep breath and tried to stop time by yelling. "Oh no!"

Nothing happened.

Kat gave Bobby a withering stare. "There's no point in shouting like a big baby."

"He must be in denial," said Teabag.

Bobby began to protest. "You don't understand..."

"I understand there's somebody coming down the corridor," gulped Kat.

The children listened to the sound of heavy footsteps as they echoed off the walls, and a deep purple light was beginning to brighten up their surroundings.

Then, from around the corner, came the most horrible looking thing that any of them had ever seen. It could only be described as a thing as it was almost ten foot tall and covered in layers of fat and hair. It had a head similar to a giant hog and it had two large tusks pointing upwards on either side of its big blubbery mouth. It was carrying a giant lantern that was giving off a bright purple light, and all it was wearing was a scruffy brown pair of pants held up with a piece of string, and a pink hat that had "Kiss Me Quick" written across it. It also had a terrible smell, even worse than somebody's feet after they've had their boots on all week.

The children were too amazed to be frightened.

Kat squirmed uncomfortably in the net. "You don't see something like this every day."

The youngsters amazement soon transformed into hysterical terror and they all began to giggle uncontrollably.

Teabag had tears of laughter running down his face. "I bet it's going to eat us all."

The children laughed even louder.

The creature snatched the net from the roof and flung it over its shoulder and headed back the way it had come.

The children bounced up and down off the creature's back as it walked and they all held their noses because of its terrible pong.

Kat's eyes started to water. "Have they never heard of deodorant down here?"

They giggled even more, but it didn't need a rocket scientist to tell them that they were in big, big trouble.

After a short distance they came to a large black door and the creature swung it open, lumbered through, and slammed it shut again. He threw them down in a corner and hung the lantern up on one of the walls.

They were inside a vast cavern with large lavender coloured flags hanging everywhere. Oddly enough, the cavern was strewn with large computers, and hung on the wall was a giant map which had little red flags stuck all over it.

The creature let them loose from the net and bellowed. "There is no escape, so don't try bothering!" It had a low stuttering hissing voice, which could only be described as a cross between a snake and a burping hippo. "I am Fatwad, Second Boss in Great Troll Army." The Troll saluted one of the lavender flags that hung from the wall.

"A Troll," Bobby whispered under his breath. "It's not every day you get captured by a Troll."

"I am Fatwad and I am hungry, and you will have the honour of being my dinner."

Kat frowned. "No, it's okay, Fatbutt."

"Fatwad!" boomed Fatwad.

"Yes, whatever," continued Kat. "I was just declining your kind offer of becoming your dinner."

"It is decided!" roared Fatwad licking its fat lips. "Fatwad eats you in half an hour." The Troll lolloped over to the computer and typed in a number of commands and then it lolloped to the giant map and stuck in another red flag.

Bobby wondered why he'd been given Superpowers if he was going to be eaten before he could ever use them. It's just typical, I'll be the shortest lived Superhero of all time, and nobody will even know I've been one, except me and my budgie.

Teabag, being a computer whizz kid, was quite interested in the Troll's activity, and even though he would be dead soon, he couldn't stop himself from saying. "I don't recognize any of these computers, but they're really really wicked. Are you playing some kind of computer game?"

The Troll lurched over to them menacingly. "You are much nosey child people. The last nosey child person wore this hat," and it pointed a chubby finger to the "Kiss Me Quick" hat perched on the top of its head. "I eat him with a good glass of red wine. But as I eat you soon I tell you the Troll Army plans." And just like any other evil villain, Fatwad told the three children how the Trolls would take over the world. "So your greenhouse effect is Troll work and your stupid moron scientists got it wrong. Us underground Trolls have been heating up all the volcanoes for years. All very hot volcanoes are on map with a red flag. The Troll computer tells us in ten of your people years, all persons on the outside of the earth will burn up and then Fatwad and all the Trolls go upstairs and live on the topside."

"But the world will be too hot for you, as well," reasoned Teabag.

"No it won't. We blow cold air up the volcanoes when human race is all dead." The big smelly Troll shook with laughter and boomed. "My belly rumbles very much and I must eat my little child people!" It moved surprisingly fast for a ten foot Troll with a pot belly, and it grabbed hold of Bobby's arm in its giant sweaty hand and lifted him to its mouth.

Kat and Teabag sprang into action and began kicking and biting the Troll's legs, but it was no use as Fatwad was far too big and strong.

Fatwad chuckled as the young boy's head entered its mouth. Bobby could smell the Troll's foul breath, and he could even see a couple of human bones stuck between its teeth the Troll slowly closed its jaws on his head. Its big sharp teeth were centimetres from his face, and Troll drool was dripping all over him as he waited helplessly for his head to be chewed right off. But the Troll didn't bite.

Bobby waited for a second or two before he wriggled out of the Troll's hand and dropped to the floor.

Kat and Teabag were perfectly still. Frozen like statues kicking at the big Troll's legs.

The enormous Troll clock on the wall had stopped

ticking.

Time had stopped once again.

Bobby had no idea how long this would last and so he acted as quickly as he could. First he picked up a giant iron poker that was leant up against the wall beside the massive black door and he rammed it into the big Troll's heart. Then he ran over to the computers and lifted the poker above his head and brought it down on them as hard as he could, but this didn't seem to have much effect. He noticed a giant red button with the words "DO NOT PRESS" written across it. The button was in a large glass case.

What the heck.

He smashed the case and pressed the button. As he did this he heard a terrible howl of pain and he turned to see Fatwad falling to the ground with thick Troll blood jetting out of its heart.

Kat and Teabag leapt out of the way as the falling Troll hit the ground with a great thud.

A mechanical voice shrieked out from a giant lavender speaker on the wall. "The Troll world will self destruct in fifty bluggs and counting!"

"What's going on?" shouted Teabag over the sound of the speaker.

Bobby shrugged. "I think I've pressed the Troll self-destruct button! We've only got fifty bluggs to get out of here!"

"How long's a blugg?"

"How the hell should I know!"

"The Troll world will self destruct in forty bluggs and counting!" wailed the loud speaker.

"Blimey," said Kat. "Bluggs are a lot quicker than seconds."

The three children ran to the giant Troll door, but it

was locked, and they didn't know where Fatwad had put the keys. It didn't matter anyway, because there were Trolls on the other side of the door and they were burning through it with lasers.

"The Troll world will self destruct in thirty bluggs and counting!"

"I wish he would belt up!" cried Kat.

The children raced back to the computers and Teabag, being the computer whizz kid, began pressing all the buttons, until one of the screens lit up with this message. "For silver fast lift to topside, press the blue button on the main Troll computer."

"The Troll world will self destruct in twenty bluggs and counting!"

The children ran to the main computer, smashed the glass case, and pressed the blue button.

The Trolls had almost burnt through the big black door.

After the blue button had been pressed, a giant silver tube rose out of the ground and a door on the tube slid open.

The Trolls were in the room.

"Get inside the tube!" cried Bobby.

They jumped inside the door as dozens of Trolls trundled across the room towards them.

"The Troll world will self destruct in ten bluggs, nine, eight, seven, six..."

The silver door slid shut and the tube shot up through a vent in the cave at such an incredible speed it flattened the children to the floor. As they were flying upwards, they could hear explosion after explosion below them.

Kat glanced at the others. "It looks like they've run out of bluggs."

The tube began to slow and then came to a halt. The

children stepped out of the silver door and found themselves in Witches Woods. They hugged each other and did a little dance of celebration.

Teabag glanced at Bobby. "How on earth did you kill Fatwad? One minute he was going to chew your head off, the next minute he was dead on the floor."

"I just got lucky," Bobby mumbled with an innocent smile.

"Who cares what happened?" said Kat. "We've saved the world from the Trolls and we can't tell a soul about it."

"Why not?" asked Teabag.

"Who do you think is going to believe us? I can hardly believe it myself."

After saying their goodbyes, the three tired children trampled their weary way home.

Bobby walked and pondered. I suppose I'm a proper Superhero now, considering I've saved the world, but, like Kat says, we can't tell anyone. As he was thinking how unfair this was, Arnie landed on his shoulder.

You left my cage open again. Have you got sawdust for brains?

"I left it open on purpose, because I don't like to think of you being locked up like a jailbird."

Thanks very much, Bobby boy, you're not a bad sort, are you?

"I suppose not, especially as I've been out saving the world tonight."

Have you been at the wine gums again?

"I'll tell you all about it later, Arnie, but right now I just want to get home and have a bath, because I'm covered in Troll spit."

Troll spit, my eye. Why can't you just admit you're a sloppy eater? I'll see you back at the house.

And off the budgie flew.

When Bobby arrived home, his family were tucking

into dinner.

Mr Coleman looked up with his mouth jammed full of roast potatoes. "Mmmppfff mnnfff snnnf mmpp."

Mrs Coleman started to translate.

Bobby interrupted. "Yes, I know, you started dinner without me because I'm late getting home."

"That's right," Mrs Coleman said in her most motherly way. "You must like cold food."

"I bet American Superheroes don't have to put up with cold food after they've just saved the world," moaned Bobby.

"I don't know what you're talking about," said Mrs Coleman. "But if Batman and Robin lived in this house, they'd have to be sat around the table dead on six o'clock just like everyone else."

"You're talking out of your hat, mum," grumbled Bobby.

"Right, upstairs!" shouted Mr Coleman. "If you can't be civil to your mother, you can get upstairs and let the rest of us finish our dinner in peace."

"It doesn't bother me," Bobby said peevishly. "I hate sprouts anyway." A few moments later Bobby lay on his bed sulking. I bet Superman never gets sent to his room. It's tough being a Superhero *and* a twelve year old boy.

Little Anna entered the room and sprang up next to him. "Why were you so late for dinner?"

"Because I've been saving the world from the Troll Army."

"Oh, I think Trolls are horrible things," Anna said with a shivery shudder.

"You're not wrong, Anna."

"You seem very down, Bobby, is there something wrong?"

Bobby sighed. "No, I'm alright, Anna. When you get

to my age, you just have a few more problems to contend with, that's all."

"I know what you mean," Anna said with a knowing smile. "Life's a lot more carefree when you're six." She got up off the bed and gave him a little kiss on the cheek before she skipped out of the room.

This made Bobby feel a lot better.

CHAPTER FOUR

ALIEN ABDUCTION

Life returned to normal in the new year. Bobby went back to school and tried to forget he was a Superhero, because no matter how many Superpowers he had, he was still bottom of the class in Mathematics. He didn't want to be the most stupid Superhero on the planet, so he studied hard at school, and though he stayed near the top of his class in most subjects, he drifted along at the bottom of the class in Maths. Well, you can't be good at everything.

The winter days gradually tumbled by, until one day Bobby embarked on his second Superadventure.

It was a cold February day and he was with Kat and Teabag in an old adventure playground on a field near to where they lived. It was a pretty sorry looking playground, and about the only adventure to be had was not treading in all the broken glass. The children were sat at the top of the slide but they couldn't slide down the thing as it was completely covered in moss.

Kat was telling the boys, for the *millionth* time, how she had destroyed the Troll world. "So against all the odds, I saved the planet from the mighty Trolls."

"Sometimes I wish the Trolls had won," sighed Teabag. "Anything to save me from hearing that pigging story ever again. You only saved the world, you know? Superman's been doing it for years."

Kat gazed up at the heavens. "You had to be there, I suppose."

"I was there, gormless."

Kat stood up and walked down the slide, and she was just about to say something very witty and clever, when a bright yellow beam shone down from above and a second later the three children were gone.

All the gathered birds gasped in amazement and burst into applause. They agreed that these children were the most entertaining the neighbourhood had ever known. They were a constant source of fun.

The three children were understandably confused, because only seconds ago they were sat at the top of the slide in a field in Milltown, and now they were somewhere else in the solar system, trapped behind a forcefield on an alien spaceship.

Teabag shrugged his shoulders. "Where are we this time?"

"Well, before anyone else says it," said Kat, "we're definitely not in Milltown anymore. In fact, I don't think we're even on the planet."

The spaceship was very gruesome indeed. All the surrounding colours seemed dull and lifeless. There were no curves or rounded edges to the spacecraft, and there were some truly terrible paintings hanging from the walls. But the most frightening part of the ship was an incredibly long shelf directly opposite the children. On this shelf there were hundreds of large jars, and pickled in these jars were the heads of some of the most unusual looking creatures you could ever imagine.

Cat-like heads. Dog-like heads. Fish-like heads. Big heads. Small heads. Blue heads. Green heads. Fat heads. Thin heads. There was even a jar with a three-headed beast inside.

"Why can't they have jars full of pickles like everybody else?" Kat said with a grimace.

"Trust us to get beamed up by inter-galactic head-hunters," moaned Teabag.

Bobby was pacing up and down. "There's no point complaining. We've got to think of a way out of here. If we can escape from the Trolls then we can escape from anything."

As the children were trying to think of a plan of action, their captors entered the room.

If you think the ten foot Troll was terrifying, then you should have seen these suckers. If you can imagine twelve foot earwigs with the teeth of a T-Rex and the talons of a giant eagle then you would be halfway to understanding how really gruesome they were. They were wearing giant silver insect suits, and they wore huge glasses with thick lenses that made their horrible red eyes seem twice the size they really were. They scampered over to the children and one of them screeched. "Earthlings, you are prisoners of the Minky army! *Resistance is futile!*"

"How come you speak English?" asked a bemused Teabag. "*Even* the French don't speak English and they only live twenty miles from England. Have you invented a universal translator, or something?"

"No, Earthling, it is just one of those strange co-incidences..."

"You're telling me it's strange," interrupted Kat. "Every time aliens attack the Earth, on telly, or in the movies, they always speak English. How come they never speak Spanish, or Japanese?"

"It is lucky for you that we don't speak Japanese, Earth creature," the terrible earwig began jabbing four of its legs at the children, "because if we did, you wouldn't understand a word we are saying. Now shut up! You Earthlings talk *too* much. You are the gobbiest race in the Universe, as well as being the ugliest. He is Zargg," the monstrous insect pointed its other four legs at Zargg, "and my name is John."

"John?" cried the children in unison. They all began to laugh.

"What is wrong with John?" asked the earwig called John.

"Nothing," they bawled.

"Why are you laughing then?"

"It's just a funny name for an alien, that's all," giggled Teabag.

"No, it is not!" snapped the earwig. "My dad was also called John."

And the children laughed even louder.

John the earwig scowled. "You Earthlings are weird." He shrugged his many shoulders. "But no matter," he continued, "we beamed you onto the ship because we need a human volunteer."

"A volunteer for what?" Teabag asked reluctantly.

The earwig called Zargg brought something from behind his back. It was a large empty jar similar to those containing all the heads. Zargg spoke for the first time. "We need a volunteer's head to fill one of these."

"Don't raise your hands all at once," said John rattling with insect laughter. "Now that's what I call real humour," he boasted. "You have one minute of your Earth time to select a volunteer."

Bobby decided to stall the insects by asking them what their plans were, because if they were anything like the Troll they would enjoy bragging about themselves. He sauntered right up to the forcefield. "What are you Minkys doing here?"

Zargg seemed very pleased that he had been asked this question. "As you Earthlings must die, I may as well tell you the Minky Army's plans to conquer the Earth."

"It works every time," whispered Bobby.

"The planet Mink is dying," Zargg continued in his gravelly insect voice. "Your Earth is very similar to our planet, and even though it's a bit too wet for our liking, it will still be quite adequate for our purposes. We are the only Minkys on this scout ship and we are here to fire our brain wave disruptors at all your world leaders. By this time tomorrow they will be under our influence and then we will send for the rest of our ships. The world leaders will tell everyone that we mean no harm, but after we have landed, we are going to have the biggest slap up meal in Minky history."

Teabag had heard enough and he shouted at the top of his voice. "You won't get away with this you big evil smelling insecty thing!"

"Oh, but I think we will," hissed Zargg making a rather rude gesture at Teabag with three of his legs. "And now I have decided to cut *all* your heads off, because you Earthlings talk *far* too much. Come John, we must go and get the head shears."

The giant earwigs crawled quickly out of the room.

Kat gazed at Teabag. "Big evil smelling insecty thing," she snorted, "where did you get *that* one from?"

"It's all I could think of at the time, and they *do* smell like bad eggs."

Bobby couldn't think straight, because the Minkys' eggy smell was putting him right off. He was trying to figure out how his Superpowers could get them out of this mess, but their foul smell had got right up his nose and was making his eyes itch. He gave his eyes a serious rub to relieve the irritation. And he promptly disappeared.

Kat had just noticed that Bobby had disappeared when the earwigs scuttled back into the room carrying the most fearsome head shears you could ever imagine.

The giant insects scuttled over to the forcefield and Zargg screeched. "Where is Earthling number Three?"

"Oh, he was feeling a bit peckish," said Teabag, "so he went home."

"What is this?" rattled Zargg, getting his antennae all in a twist. "Tell us where he is or we will come in there and sit on you until you do."

"You'll have to catch us first, beetle face," taunted Kat.

"Right, that's it," squeaked John. "You Earthlings give me the hump. Let's see how cocky you are with a great big Minky sitting on top of you. Lower the forcefield, Zargg."

Zargg dropped the forcefield and as the earwigs scurried into the prison, the invisible boy zipped out.

Bobby wasn't sure how long he would stay invisible so he had to be quick. He picked up the two head shears that the insects had put on the far shelf and ran back to the prison.

Zargg had Teabag in a headlock and the other earwig was positioning his big insect backside over him.

Kat was crouched in the corner and she knew that the weight of the earwig would kill Teabag. Things looked hopeless, but she wasn't going to sit there and watch Teabag die. She stood up and got ready to fight. Then to her complete surprise she saw the two head shears floating towards her. She blinked her eyes, but she wasn't seeing things. She was totally baffled, but this didn't stop her grabbing a pair of the shears when they were within reach.

Just as the two earwigs were about to crush the life out of Teabag, two large head shears were placed around their necks and Snap! Snap! the earwigs massive heads were sent crashing to the floor.

Teabag rolled away from the collapsing earwigs as litres of sticky green blood spurted out of their headless bodies.

Bobby had become visible again, and he booted one of the giant earwig heads clear across the room.

Teabag applauded. "Good shot!"

Kat put her hands on Bobby's shoulders. "Where the flipping heck have you been?"

"I'll tell you later," he replied. "We're not out of trouble yet."

The children ran through the door that the insects had come through, and legged it down an ink coloured corridor that led to the flight deck. There was a bank of computers along one wall and a flight control panel at the front of the ship. The spaceship window was dominated by the gigantic moon.

"Where's the Earth gone?" gasped Kat.

"We're on the dark side of the moon," said Teabag, who was now sat in front of the Minky computers trying to figure out how they worked.

Bobby was sat in the pilot's seat and he pushed the yellow metal wheel that was right in front of him. The ship lurched forward and he yelled to the others. "I'm going to fly this to Earth. Try and find out what you can from all the Minky computers."

"Aye aye, Captain," Teabag said with a mad giggle. "This is just like being in Star Trek." Teabag found a transmitter in the computer bank and sent a message to the Minky planet saying that Earth was unsuitable for Minky life as the atmosphere was methane, and that the two space earwigs were heading off to search for more suitable planets. Teabag grinned at Kat. "They'll never know I was lying about the methane."

As the space ship hurtled towards Earth, Bobby raised his eyes from the control panels. "Does anyone know where the brakes are?"

Nobody did.

The three adventurers had bravely killed the aliens and saved the world from being over run by giant earwigs and now they were hurtling towards the planet at close to the speed of light. They hugged each other and said their farewells, for in a matter of seconds they would all be dead as the spacecraft sped closer and closer to an almighty collision with the earth.

Teabag looked at the computer. "I wonder what this yellow button does?"

"Why don't you press it and find out?" said Kat.

"Why not, indeed." Teabag pressed the yellow button.

The three children floated down to the Milltown adventure playground in the rays of the weird yellow beam. They jigged around with joy.

Teabag suddenly stopped jigging and pointed to the heavens. "Look at that go."

Streaking through the atmosphere, far over their heads, was an unusual yellow object that resembled a meteorite, but our three heroes knew what it really was.

"Bye bye, Minkys!" yelled Teabag waving his hand.

Kat gazed up at the stars. "That's another adventure we're going to have to keep to ourselves. When are we going to go on an adventure that people will believe?" She stopped gazing at the stars and glanced at Bobby. "And by the way, how did you manage the vanishing act?"

"It's all done with mirrors," Bobby replied as he started to walk back home.

The children parted and went their separate ways.

Bobby walked and wondered. That's twice I've saved the world with a little help from my friends. I wonder if the American Superheroes know that I'm out there doing what they're supposed to do? And where exactly have they been while I've been saving the planet? Probably sat on their big Superbottoms watching one of their own movies on the telly. I'm beginning to think I'm the only Superhero doing any work, and nobody even knows I'm doing it.

He was feeling very hard done by, when Arnie landed on his Supershoulder.

Why are you looking so down in the dumps?

"Oh, it's nothing Arnie, I'd just like some appreciation from time to time."

I appreciate you, Bobby boy.

"No disrespect, Arnie, but I mean for other things."

What other things?

"Oh, just little things, like saving the world every now and again."

You're not going to start that again are you?

"No, I'm not. I just want to get home, have a bath, and wash all this green alien blood off me."

I was wondering what that was. I thought someone had thrown up on you. So it's alien blood is it? You keep taking the pills and I'll see you back at the house.

As Bobby strolled slowly home he knew he couldn't tell the world he'd saved the planet from Trolls and Minkys as even his budgie didn't believe him. He stepped in a puddle that came up to his ankles and soaked his brand new trainers. So that's the thanks I get for my troubles, is it? Well, that's the *last* time I save *this* planet.

CHAPTER FIVE

TARQUIN McWHACKER

Tarquin McWhacker lived in a vast castle. He was so evil he couldn't even be bothered to learn the name of the place where he lived. It was called Millsomethingorother. Every time he tried to remember the name some evil thought would come into his head and that would be that. Tarquin also had incredible Superpowers.

He would have been a Superhero but for his name. Fancy being called Tarquin McWhacker. He was teased quite relentlessly at every school he attended and, as his dad was a travelling salesman, he went to a fair few. But no matter how many schools he went to he never met anyone with a more silly name than his. The teasing wasn't *that* bad, but Tarquin had a bitter heart, and he imagined it to be a lot worse than it really was. So his bitterness grew and grew and grew.

Then one day, as Tarquin was walking by a canal throwing rocks at the fish, up jumped a rabid, radioactive Canal Goblin and bit him on the leg. This was very unlucky indeed, even for somebody called Tarquin McWhacker.

The next day was his sixteenth birthday, and he woke up with incredible Superpowers. Should he be good or should he be evil? The answer was easy.

Tarquin had been bitten by a rabid, radioactive Canal Goblin and he had inherited four Superpowers. These Superpowers were nearly all water based, because he'd been bitten by a water dwelling Goblin. These are the powers he now possessed: Superpower One – he could hold his breath under water for three months. Superpower Two – he could swim twice as fast as a dolphin. Superpower Three – he could catch and eat a fly in 0.2 seconds. Superpower Four – his brain waves had been boosted a million times over, making him a mathematical genius with incredible hypnotic powers.

Tarquin left home, stole billions of pounds and bought himself a castle in Millwhatdoyoucallit.

He became a billionaire by using his vastly improved mathematical brain to hack into bank computers all over the world and transfer their money into his own account.

When he first moved to wherever it was he lived, he only did slightly evil things as he was still finding his feet. He would throw banana skins under joggers' feet, he would show pictures of cooked lamb to sheep, and he would tell five year olds that Santa didn't exist. But he knew he was destined for greater things than this and it wasn't long before he was doing truly evil things. Surely there can be nobody more evil than a teenager who will go on his holidays to Africa just to tell all the lions where the gnus were hiding. He was so evil he invented a pill that would give goldfish long memories, and when you live in a goldfish bowl, the last thing you want is a memory longer than seven seconds.

Tarquin decided it was time for a change. He wanted a new name like all the American Superheroes had. He spent hours thinking of different names. Slug Boy – too slimy. Evil Boy – too obvious. Naughty Boy – too boring. After six hours ten minutes and five seconds he came up with the perfect name.

Tarquin McWhacker was dead. Long live the Shadow.

By the time he was sixteen and a half, the Shadow was the most evil teenager the world had ever seen. Soon he would put his evil plans into action, but not quite yet.

For the time being, the Shadow was content to wait in the shadows.

CHAPTER SIX

BROTHER M

It was a lovely spring day in Milltown. Bobby was on his way home from school, and as it was a Tuesday he decided to go to Witches Woods after tea and say hello to Thelma. As he was wandering home, he was thinking about his power of invisibility. Over the last few weeks he had discovered that if he rubbed his eyes he became invisible, but he also found that if he tried to do this too often the power became unreliable, and so he decided to use this power only when he was in real trouble. As he walked down his garden path, Arnie fluttered over and landed on his shoulder.

Welcome home, Master.

"Hello Arnie," he said. "And stop calling me Master. It's embarrassing."

Your wish is my command.

As he was passing through the hallway he said to his budgie. "Do you want to come and see Thelma with me tonight?"

I'll have to think about that for a second... Er, no can do, I'm playing croquet with the sparrows tonight.

Though the thought of sparrows and budgies playing croquet might seem peculiar, nobody really knows what birds get up to in their spare time.

Bobby walked into the dining room where his family were settling down to eat.

Mr Coleman gawped at him. "Is there something

wrong with your watch?"

"My watch is working perfectly, thank you for asking. I just thought I would try hot food for a change." He commenced wolfing down his food.

Mr Coleman watched him eat for a few seconds. "If you ate a bit slower, you might be able to taste your food."

"Maybe I don't want to taste my food," Bobby said with a cheeky smirk.

"We will have less of that, young man," snapped Mrs Coleman. "Or you'll be making your own tea in future."

"Sorry mum, it's very tasty, whatever it is."

Bobby had searched all over the woods, but he couldn't find Thelma or her green fire. "I'm sure she said Tuesdays and Thursdays," he said to himself as he sat on a log wondering where the witch could be.

Arnie soared over the trees and landed next to him on the log.

"I thought you were playing croquet with the sparrows?"

A magpie ate the croquet balls.

The pair sat on the log in silence for a couple of minutes, until Arnie looked up from preening his feathers.

By the way, there's a stranger in a white suit heading this way.

"It's not Thelma, is it?"

Wearing a white suit? I don't think so. Anyhow, it's a man.

At that moment a stranger in a white suit approached and when he noticed the boy sitting on the log he paused. "I am Brother Martin, but you can call me Brother M. I am wondering why you are so deep in these woods, as I hear they have quite a supernatural reputation."

"I'm exercising my budgie," said Bobby. "And if the woods have such a reputation then why are you here?"

"Good question, young man," said the curious person in the white suit. "I am a weather expert and a storm chaser and I hear there have been some unusual storms in this region recently."

Bobby remembered the weird thunder and lightning that Thelma had conjured up when creating his budgie. He wondered what other strange weather conditions the witches had caused when performing their magic.

Brother Martin was waffling on about clouds and rain and thunder and light showery intervals, but Bobby wasn't really listening to him as he had one of those dull monotonous voices that send you to sleep five minutes after you've just woken up.

Arnie let out a tiny little yawn.

This bloke's draining my will to live.

He flew off to explore.

Brother Martin was still droning on at a fair old pace, "...and so I am particularly interested in cloud formation and precipitation."

"Pre cippy what?" asked Bobby.

"Precipitation, or rainfall, if you prefer," explained Brother Martin. "Don't they teach you anything at school?"

As Bobby was thinking of a cutting reply, Arnie swooped back over the trees with a worried expression on his face.

Ask him if he's lost a white handkerchief.

Bobby was confused, but he did as he was told. "Have you lost a white handkerchief, Brother M?"

Brother Martin checked the breast pocket of his white suit. "Why yes, I have, but how could you know that?"

Arnie twittered out loud.

He's killed Thelma. I found her dead by the old oak tree, and there's a white handkerchief by her side. You'd better get out of here quick.

53

Arnie disappeared over the trees.

Brother Martin frowned. "I know where I might have dropped it. Follow me."

"What if I don't want to?" asked Bobby.

"I am not *asking* you, I am *telling* you," growled Brother Martin.

"Who do you think *you* are?"

"I think I am Brother Martin and you must obey me."

"Obey you!" cried Bobby. "You sound like a flipping Dalek."

Brother Martin pulled out a silver hand gun and pointed it at the boy.

"Isn't that a bit radical," gulped Bobby. "You can't shoot someone just because they won't do as you tell them. If you don't put that away I'll set my budgie on you. Don't be fooled by his size."

Brother Martin stood there and said nothing.

This was beginning to irritate Bobby a bit. He didn't want to risk becoming invisible by rubbing his eyes, as he thought this crazy man might shoot him if he made any sudden movements, and as time hadn't stopped yet, he decided to throw the man off guard by saying. "I know that you've killed a witch."

Brother Martin finally broke his silence. "You are a very curious young man, aren't you?" He had a strange glint in his eye. "How did you know that I'd lost my handkerchief? And how did you know I've killed a witch? Are you a little wizard?"

Bobby shook his head. The man in the white suit wasn't taking the bait and so he decided to try another angle of attack. "You look like an advert for Supersuds."

Brother Martin seemed a little confused by this and then it clicked. "Oh, I get it, you mean the white suit. Very good." Then he lifted the gun up and grinned. "It's time to

54

blow your head off."

"Wait! Wait!" yelled Bobby. "At least tell me why you're going to kill me."

"Because I intend to rule the world."

Bobby sighed. "Not another one."

"Oh yes, I will kill all mankind." Brother Martin was becoming more and more animated. "Do you wish to know how I shall do this?

Bobby made a little yawning noise. "Not really."

"You *will* listen!" screamed Brother Martin. "Or I will blow your head off right now."

"I'm all ears," said Bobby, sitting up straight.

Brother Martin walked up and down as he spoke. "Witches Woods is the perfect location for my experiment with the world's weather. In ten days time, my nine accomplices and I will explode a gas bomb in the clouds releasing a cocktail of chemicals. After this there will be a chain reaction and every time it rains it will be acid rain."

"That won't to do the world much good."

"Exactly," Brother Martin said with a sly grin, "but you haven't heard the best part yet."

"I've got a funny feeling I'm about to."

"After a year of acid rain, all the seas and rivers will be poisoned and all the animals will slowly die and the human race will starve to death."

"Forgive me if I seem a bit dim here, but won't you starve as well?"

"Oh, I will be fine. For I am not what I seem to be." Brother Martin paused for a few seconds. He seemed to be lost in a world of his own. He snapped out of his daydreams. "I have told you all you need to know, little wizard. It's time for you to die."

"If I've only got a year to live, why kill me now?"

"Oh, this is just for fun!" Brother Martin cried with a

crazy look in his eyes. "Say your goodbyes, little wizard." He lifted the gun and squeezed the trigger.

Arnie came swooping out of the clouds like a little spitfire and dive bombed the man in the white suit colliding with his hand just as he was about to shoot, and then he swept back over the trees again.

The bullet from the gun whizzed over Bobby's head and he seized the opportunity to escape. He spun on his heels and ran. It wasn't long before he reached the castle that marked the end of the woods. He ran across the drawbridge with Brother Martin closing in fast, and in an act of sheer desperation, he jumped to one side and stuck out his leg.

The man in the white suit was running so fast he couldn't stop himself tripping over Bobby's leg, and he flew off the bridge and into the moat. Brother Martin bellyflopped into the water and then swam back to the bridge and hauled himself out. He stood there dripping with water, and then, quite unexpectedly, blue smoke poured out of his eyes and ears and nostrils. "Not the water! Not the water! We are so close! Kill them all! I am a pretty tomato! I live in a pink cup, my Aunty is a wildebeest..." then his head blew right off his shoulders. His body carried on jumping up and down and shaking its fists and there were wires and electronic components protruding out of his neck.

"He's a flipping robot!" cried Bobby in surprise.

Brother Martin stopped dancing around and came to a standstill. He stood there like a statue, minus its head, with thousands of sparks fizzing out of his neck.

Then the portcullis to the castle began to lift with a loud grating noise. Inside a room at the top of the castle, a shadowy figure sat over the controls that worked the portcullis.

Bobby knew it wasn't such a good idea to enter this dark castle, but he wanted to find out who had lifted the portcullis.

I wouldn't go in there if I were you.

Bobby almost jumped out of his skin and he glared at Arnie. "I wish you wouldn't sneak up on me like that."

I'm sorry, I happen to be a very good sneaker.

"Well, don't do it when I'm creeping into a big spooky castle, okay."

Don't go in then.

"Put a sock in it, Arnie, I need to concentrate."

I'm not going in there. When was the last time you saw a budgie in a haunted castle? I'll tell you when. Never. Because we're not that stupid. I'm off home.

Bobby stood there with his hands on his hips. "You mean you're going to go fly back through Witches Woods all on your own?"

Arnie flew into the castle.

What are you waiting for? Christmas.

CHAPTER SEVEN

THE SHADOW

The castle was very depressing. It was cold and bare and damp. It was also incredibly gloomy as there were only a few torches flickering away on the walls.

Haven't the owners heard of electricity?

"Ssshh, I want to concentrate."

This is like being back in the dark ages.

"Will you stop thinking things," hissed Bobby.

I can't help it, it's too quiet in here.

"Well try stopping, will you!" screamed Bobby. He winced as his screaming voice went echoing down the corridors.

I'm not taking any more of this abuse. Are you always this aggressive after blowing up a robot?

The budgie glided off, whistling under his breath.

Bobby found himself at the bottom of some stone stairs which he promptly decided to climb.

The young boy reached a dark room at the top of the highest turret and he went inside. In the inky shadows of the room he could just make out the shape of something coming towards him.

The shape came into view as it stepped into the light from the dark red candles high up on the wall. It was a boy of about sixteen years old. He was slightly built and dressed from head to toe in black. He carried a long black cane which had a gold handle shaped in the form of a panther. He stood quietly before Bobby, taking a few flies from the palm of his hand and putting them into his mouth. After he had swallowed the last fly, he spoke in a gentle, steady voice. "I am the Shadow, welcome to my domain."

"Er, hello, my name's Bobby Coleman," he said politely. "And you're the Shadow are you? That's an unusual name. Haven't you got a proper one?"

"Shadow is my proper name."

"No, I mean a proper name like Andy, or Dave, or Graham, or Tarquin..."

"Shut up, fool!" barked the Shadow. "I shall rule the world one day, so you better speak to me with a little more respect."

"Blimey," said Bobby. And he wondered why he never met ordinary run of the mill people instead of fly crunching maniacs like the Shadow. But he still had to deal with this character. "Just *how*, exactly, are you going to rule the world?"

"I will rule the world because I am the Shadow and I have incredible Superpowers."

"It's a small world," said Bobby.

The Shadow totally ignored what Bobby had said. "Soon the world will worship at my feet," he said as he strolled around the room making sweeping gestures with his arms. "My plans are almost ready. Nobody will ever laugh at Tarquin McWhacker again."

Bobby snorted with laugher. "Tarquin McWhacker? Who's he when he's at home?"

"Be quiet you fool!" shrieked the Shadow.

"And quit calling me a fool, will you? Only my teachers get to call me that." Bobby was very irritated by the pompous Shadow and he decided he had seen enough. "It was nice meeting you, Mr Shadow, but seeing as you've been at the loopy juice, I think I'd better be on my way." As he walked towards the stairs an iron door crashed down blocking the way out.

"Going somewhere?" said the Shadow.

"Look, Shadow!" cried Bobby. "You're not the only idiot trying to take over the world, and if I don't do something about a bunch of mechanical madmen, there won't be any world left for you to take over."

The Shadow regarded him with sly eyes. "Do you think I am foolish enough to believe your lies?"

Bobby pointed out of the castle window. "I've just killed a robot out there, that's if you can kill a robot, and there are nine more of them and they want to drown the world in acid rain."

"That's a very likely story," mocked the Shadow.

Bobby was becoming even more irritated. "I don't really care whether you believe me or not, because in ten days time, like it or not, you're going to need more than an umbrella to keep off the rain."

The Shadow thought about this for a while as he was chewing on a few more flies. "As I witnessed you destroy the robot on my monitors I will give you the benefit of the doubt. What do you suggest we do?"

"I suggest you stop eating those flies for a start," Bobby said with a little shudder.

"Ah yes, the flies," said the Shadow licking his lips. "Full of protein, you know."

"Try eating sausages," Bobby suggested. "They're bursting with protein."

"Maybe so," said the Shadow, "but I like the way the flies wriggle in my mouth."

Bobby's face turned a sickly shade of green.

Nine robots were gathered outside the castle. They had homed in on the distress signal of Brother Martin. His destruction did not bother them as they had no emotions, but they had computed that their plans were not running as efficiently as they ought to, and this made their oil boil.

Brother Jeff was the second in command. He strolled up and down in front of the other robots with his hands behind his back like some general in front of his troops. He spoke in a low monotone voice. "Fellow robots, the human that burnt out Brother Martin's diodes is in that castle. I have him on my radar. It is time for him to cease being. Follow me."

The robots had been invented by a techno-genius named Dr Rust, and he had also invented a chip that could be activated in the robot's brain. This chip allowed the robots to think for themselves, but once that happened, they decided they wanted the world for themselves. Why share the world, they computed? Once it was theirs they would carry on Dr Rust's work and build a whole new robot population.

Right now though, it was time for some robotic revenge.

CHAPTER EIGHT

ROBOT WARS

Inside the castle, the Shadow approached his computer monitor and a crooked grin appeared on his lips. "Ah, I see that our robotic friends have found us. If you stay out of the way, I will deal with these tin cans in no time at all."

The nine robots climbed the turret staircase and approached the iron door.

Brother Jeff ripped it off its hinges and stepped into the room. He sneered at the two boys. "Cowering behind iron doors isn't going to help you."

It was the Shadow's incredible hypnotic powers that made him dismiss the threat of the robots so arrogantly, because he felt he could gain control over anyone in a fraction of a second. There was just one thing the Shadow had overlooked. You cannot hypnotise a machine. So after the Shadow had tried and failed to hypnotise the robots, he transformed back into the tearful, cowardly Tarquin McWhacker and crawled under the nearest table.

Bobby was no coward though, and he stood and faced the robots, ready for a battle.

The nine robots reached up to their faces and tore off their human masks to reveal chromium skulls with bright scarlet red eyes. They signalled each other electronically and they all charged at once.

Fear rose in Bobby's terrified heart as he got ready to spring out of their way.

And time stopped.

Bobby finally realised that fear was the key. Every time he had been truly terrified time had stopped. But he couldn't dwell on that now, because he had nine robots to destroy. He had just enough time to immerse an empty bucket into the Shadow's tank of piranhas and pour the water down the throats of six of the robots, before time started ticking once again.

The six waterlogged robots began whirring around and spitting out sparks and after a few seconds blue smoke poured from their ears.

Six down, three to go.

Brother Jeff glared at him with disdain. His blood red eyes were glinting in the candlelight. "For the termination of my Brothers, I will surgically remove your head and suck out your brains."

The six malfunctioning machines grabbed the two robots next to Brother Jeff and tore them apart.

Brother Jeff was now the only robot still intact and he crouched like a cat and sprang for Bobby's throat.

The youngster rubbed his eyes and disappeared.

Brother Jeff looked around for the boy. The robot was having problems computating this data, because this defied all logic.

Bobby dodged past the robot and picked up the Shadow's black cane.

Brother Jeff spun around searching for the boy, only to see the cane heading towards him like a spear. But he had no time to react. The golden panther handle pierced his silver chest, damaging all the robot's major components. Bolts of silver lightning forked out from his metallic heart, and a fountain of oily fluid pumped out from his gaping chest. The damaged robot called out in an eerie hollow voice. "All humans must be disconnected! Robots are efficiency! Kill all humans! Kill them all! Crispy bacon, crispy bacon..." The stricken robot burned fiercely and soon a silver metallic skeleton was all that was left.

Bobby reappeared and scanned the room. All nine robots were silent and still. The planet had been saved from acid rain.

After the battle was over, the Shadow crawled from under a table and pressed a button on his computer.

A trap door slid open beneath Bobby's feet and he plummeted through it and crashed down into the dungeons below.

Two minutes later, the Shadow appeared in the dungeon and walked over to the prison cell that Bobby had landed in. He stared through the prison bars. "I'm glad to see my ingenious plan worked."

"Was that the plan where you hid under a table until the fight was over?"

"Exactly so," said the Shadow nodding. "It lulled the robots into a false sense of security and after that, you had the easy task of destroying them." He gripped one of the prison bars with his slender fingers and leant a little closer. "I did notice that you used some unusual tactics to kill the robots. Are you some kind of Superhero?"

"Well, that's the third time I've saved the world. I suppose that qualifies me for Superhero status."

"What is your name?" asked the Shadow.

"Bobby Coleman, but you already know that."

"I mean, what is your Superhero name?"

"I haven't got one."

"Oh, you must get one soon," drooled the Shadow. "It's the best part of being a Superhero. Why don't you join forces with me? You could be my assistant. We could be like an evil Batman and Robin. We could steal some of the limelight from those vomit-like American Superheroes." He wrinkled his nose in disgust. "When I rule the world that lot will be the first up against the wall." The Shadow mimed a machine gun firing. He smirked and leant even closer to the prison bars and whispered. "Become evil like me and we will rule the world together."

"Sorry Shadow, I can't just become evil, and I'm not sure I want all the glory the American Superheroes get. I'm going to have to decline your kind offer. Why don't you stop being evil and join forces with me?"

"It works both ways, Coleman," sighed the Shadow. "I can't just become good. I was born to be evil. Ah well, such is life. Now I must kill you as you are a threat to my evil plans." As the Shadow left the dungeons he pulled down a lever attached to the wall and as he swept through the dungeon door he called back over his shoulder.

"Goodbye Coleman, and thanks for killing the robots. And, by the way, I hope your cell isn't *too* small." He gave a loud diabolical laugh and slammed the dungeon door behind him.

Bobby was left all alone in the dark spooky dungeon and after a short while he realised the prison cell was getting smaller. The walls were slowly closing in and he was going to be crushed to death. The walls relentlessly edged towards him until he was only centimetres from an agonising death. This time he really was doomed, and he could think of better ways to die than this.

Are you looking for these?

There was just enough space for Bobby to turn his head towards the dungeon window.

Perched on the sill with a bunch of keys in his beak was his little green budgie.

"Quick Arnie, don't mess around, I've not long left."

Arnie flew past him and inserted one of the keys in the lock.

I want a brand new mirror in my cage after this.

"Anything Arnie, but hurry."

The key did not open the lock. Neither did the next one. The wall was now touching the youngster's nose.

The next key didn't open the door either.

I hope I've brought the right keys.

Bobby was almost out of time when the prison door finally clicked open and he was fired out of the cell like a bullet from a gun.

"Thanks, Arnie," he gasped as he slid by on his stomach. "Any longer and I would have been Pancake Boy, the flat Superhero." He slid on a little more and then slowly came to a halt. He got up and dusted himself down. "We're not out of this yet."

You might not be, but I can just fly out of the dungeon window. I've done my bit. Bye bye.

Arnie disappeared through the dungeon window.

Bobby decided he would strangle his budgie later, but first he had to get out of the dungeon. He sneaked up to the dungeon door and fortunately it had been left unlocked. He crept out of the dungeon and ran through the castle towards the drawbridge.

He would have to deal with the Shadow later, as right now this twelve year old boy had to get home and finish tomorrow's Chemistry homework.

The Shadow returned to the dungeon with a machine gun and a couple of hand grenades, as he didn't want to take any chances. He approached the prison cell where he had left Bobby to be crushed, and when he discovered what had happened he screamed. "Noooo!"

All the birds in Witches Woods awoke. A starling rubbed some sleep from her eyes with her wings and warbled to one of her friends. "Did you just hear a very loud scream of utter desperation?"

"Go back to sleep," tweeted her sleepy friend. "We've got to get up at dawn."

CHAPTER NINE

FIRE

The next morning Bobby awoke and got ready for school. He knew he would have to do something about the Shadow as his plans for taking over the world had to be taken seriously. But whatever he decided to do would have to wait until after school, because he wasn't bunking off, no matter how many evil villains wanted to conquer the planet.

He sat down at the breakfast table with Anna. His parents were upstairs getting ready for work.

Arnie was perched on his bowl of cornflakes taking a drink of milk.

"I wish you wouldn't do that," complained Bobby.

Don't be so stingy. How much do you think a budgie can drink? You should try drinking dusty water all the time.

"Why don't you do something useful for a change and go and find out what the Shadow is doing?"

Anna stopped crunching her way through her cornflakes. "Are you talking to me?"

"No Anna, I'm talking to feather brain, over here."

"I didn't know you could talk to the animals. Are you like Dr Doolittle?"

"I suppose I am, in a way."

"Will you ask Arnie where budgies come from, because I've never seen one outside our house?"

Bobby tapped the little budgie on the head. "Where

do budgies come from, Arnie?"

How should I know? I was zapped here by a witch. Why do six year olds ask so many difficult questions? Tell her I come from Poland, maybe that'll shut her up.

"I'll do no such thing," said Bobby shaking his head. He looked at his little sister. "He hasn't got a clue where budgies come from, but I can tell you where this one's going." He flicked the budgie off the table. "Get your feathers into gear and go find the Shadow." He stood up and threw his school satchel over his shoulder.

I'm going, I'm going, keep your hair on. I'll find the Shadow for you and then I will shadow him, ha ha ha. A little budgie humour for you there.

Arnie flew off and crashed straight into the window with a thud. He dropped to the carpet like a lead balloon. He lay there dazed, before standing up and retrieving one or two feathers that had fallen out during his descent. He was still a little stunned as he glared at Bobby and squawked with anger.

Who shut that window? Was it you, you great wazzock?

"No, it wasn't," Bobby replied as he opened the front door. "Perhaps you'll watch where you're going in future."

The budgie soared over him and dropped a little message on his shoulder to remind him how angry he was.

Bobby wiped the message off his shoulder with his handkerchief and shouted something after the budgie.

Arnie couldn't hear what he had shouted, but he was sure it was pretty unpleasant.

The final lesson on a Wednesday was Chemistry with Mr Baker, who was affectionately known as Laptop, because he wore a daft orange wig.

Bobby wasn't so hot at Chemistry, so he always sat with Kat and Teabag who excelled at the subject.

Today they were learning some of the properties of the elements from the periodic table. All the bunsen burners were flickering away and the class were split up into small groups.

Bobby didn't know it, but he was about to discover another Superpower.

As Teabag placed a strip of manganese into the bunsen burner flame, Bobby let out a loud cough and the flame from the bunsen burner erupted like a volcano. The flame grew bigger and bigger as it raced across the table top straight for Mr Baker.

The whole class held their breath as the flames shot across the Chemistry teacher's head and set fire to a globe of the world that was standing right behind him.

The world was slowly melting behind Mr Baker's back as he sat in front of the class with his wig on fire.

The teacher was too stunned to realise that something was burning on the top of his head.

Somebody shouted from the back of the class. "Sir, your wig's on fire!"

"What are you talking about, Perkins?" boomed the indignant teacher. "I don't wear a wig."

"Okay Sir," cried Perkins, thinking on his feet, "there's a little orange hamster burning on your head."

Mr Baker jumped up and ran to the sink and plunged his head in a bowl of water and what emerged from the bowl a couple of moments later was a very sorry sight indeed. He stood before the class with a peculiar black blob on his head. His face was a smudgy mixture of burnt ashes and water, and he was slowly turning lobster red with anger.

The class were frozen in anticipation.

Mr Baker roared louder than anyone has ever roared before. "Coleman! You are in detention! Forever!!!"

After school Bobby was sat in the detention room writing his five hundred lines. He could feel Laptop's eyes burning through his skull as he scribbled for the tenth time, "I deeply regret setting my Chemistry teacher's head on fire and burning off all his golden locks of hair." Only another four hundred and ninety to go. The teacher's head was still sending tiny smoke signals into the air and Bobby didn't dare look at him in case he burst out laughing. As he wrote down the lines, he was wondering how he could use this new Superpower to his advantage, as it might prove useful being a human flame thrower.

After he had written a couple more lines, Arnie glided in through the window and landed on his desk. He ruffled his feathers to remove a few drops of rain that had fallen on them.

I've been searching for you everywhere. Don't speak, or you'll attract the teacher's attention. Blimey, what's happened to his head... Right, I found the Shadow and he's still working on his plan for world domination, so there's no need to worry about him for a while. But there is something very strange happening in Witches Woods. You haven't got time to finish detention.

Bobby nodded to show that he understood and then he gave his eyes a little rub.

Mr Baker was marking some class work when he heard footsteps in the classroom. He looked up from his desk to find the boy had disappeared, although he did notice a little green budgie flying up from the desk where he'd been sat. The teacher listened carefully to the footsteps walking towards him and then the door to the classroom opened and closed right before his eyes. He knew he must be seeing things after the shock of having his head set on fire. But where had Coleman gone? The teacher growled under his breath. "Wait until I get hold of that sneaky little brat. I'll make him wish he'd never been born." He stood up and went to search for the missing boy, muttering over and over. "I'll get you for this Coleman, if it's the last thing I ever do."

CHAPTER TEN

WORM HOLE

Bobby was still invisible as he passed his mum on the street. "Hello mum, I'll be a bit late for tea," he called as he ran by.

Mrs Coleman almost jumped out of her skin. She looked around, but there was nobody there. "I'll have to see a doctor if I keep hearing these voices," she mumbled to herself.

A couple of minutes later Bobby became visible again and he bumped into Kat and Teabag.

"Shouldn't you be in detention?" asked Kat.

"Change of plans. Follow me."

Kat and Teabag didn't have time to ask him any questions. So they tagged on behind him, climbed the red iron gates and jumped into Witches Woods.

Arnie was perched in a nearby elm tree.

You're not going to believe what I've found. Follow me.

The children ran after the budgie into the deepest part of the woods, where even the witches didn't go.

Arnie fluttered up into the branches of a yew tree and pointed his left wing in a northerly direction.

Take a look over there.

The children glanced northwards and they were astounded by a sight that was stranger than anything they had seen for at least, oh, twenty four hours.

The bushes and the trees were all perfectly normal,

72

apart from a circular area about eight feet in diameter. In this area, all the trees and bushes lost their shape, and it was if they were being whirled around in a giant green washing machine.

Teabag had seen countless science fiction movies, and so he said, with great authority. "It's a worm-hole."

"A worm what?" said Kat.

"A short cut between one place in the universe and another." explained Teabag. "And worm-holes can also be used to travel backwards or forwards in time."

"Oh, one of them," nodded Kat, pretending to understand.

Whilst they stood there admiring the view, out popped a man and a woman.

The two newcomers were quite small and very ordinary looking. They wore clothes made from grey satin, and they were carrying tiny crystals in their hands.

The female said. "I am Zis and this is Zat. We are from the year 3777. We are dreamtakers and have been using the worm-hole for many years."

"What are dreamtakers?" asked Teabag.

"We collect other peoples' dreams," Zis replied, "because, in the future, the leaders of the world have removed the gene that makes people dream."

"Why would they do that?" asked Kat.

"Because they are cruel and terrible people," said Zis. "There are six dictators who govern Upper England and they call themselves the Masters. They had to fight a long bloody war to gain power, and now they rule the future through death and destruction. After the war they decided that people without dreams would be easier to control. So we don't dream anymore and they have absolute power."

"This is why we come back in time to take your dreams. We collect as many as we can and take them back in our crystals," explained Zat.

Bobby frowned. "Isn't it wrong to take peoples' dreams?"

"It is a harmless procedure," said Zis. "We never take more than one dream off a person, and when we get back to the future we use these dreams to lift our spirits. This helps us to carry on our crusade against the Masters, but we are fighting a losing battle, because we cannot gather enough dreams to sustain our small army."

Kat pointed at the worm-hole. "Isn't that thing dangerous?"

"We always close the worm-hole after we leave," said Zat. "These woods have very magical qualities and it is the only place in England where we can get through. It has not caused any problems up to now."

Bobby gazed at the whirring worm-hole. "Can we come through the worm-hole with you? Perhaps we can help you defeat the Masters, then you will be able to close the worm-hole forever."

"The Masters are all powerful and you would be killed," said Zis.

"At least we could try."

Teabag was looking very very worried. "Could you repeat the bit about us being killed?"

Zat bowed his head slightly towards Bobby. "We will let you try if you so wish."

Arnie swooped down and landed on Bobby's shoulder and ruffled up his feathers with pride.

I'm going to be the first time travelling budgie. This is one small step for a man, one giant leap for budgie kind.

The three children and the budgie followed Zis and Zat into the worm-hole. They were all subjected to the unusual sensation of travelling through time. It was like riding on a rollercoaster while drinking a glass of water standing on your head and having your feet tickled with feathers.

They stepped through the worm-hole once they reached the other side and took in their new surroundings.

"Welcome to your future," Zis said with a large sweep of her arm.

And what a horrible future it was. For the future was grey. Everywhere was grey. Up and down, left and right. Grey, grey, grey.

"It's a bit grey, isn't it?" said Teabag.

Bobby stared at all the concrete. "What's happened to Witches Woods?"

"The Masters tore all the woodlands down, because they said beautiful places were too inspiring," explained Zat. "Where wooded areas once stood, now there is only concrete. We will take you to the Masters' castle."

"Please do," said Bobby, "I can't wait to meet them."

They walked down street after street, and each one they went down was as grey and depressing as the last one. It was so depressing that after a while even the sunlight seemed grey.

After a short while they reached the castle, which was the same one next to Witches Woods back in the past. But the castle of the future had changed. This one was covered in pure gold and encrusted with diamonds and rubies.

Kat snorted with disgust. "I see the Masters don't live in a concrete house."

"The Masters enjoy living in luxury," said Zis.

"The castle is guarded by soldiers and laden with booby traps," said Zat, "but there is an underground passage that will take you as far as the old dungeon. We will take you to the entrance and then you will be on your own."

Zis and Zat stood at the entrance of the passage and wished the children luck.

Zat spoke. "We will wait here until nightfall and if you are not back by then you will be dead."

"Oh, we'll be back," promised Kat.

The young time travellers stepped into the passage and then they jumped straight back out again.

"Cor, it's a bit dark in there!" exclaimed Teabag.

"Have you got a torch or something?" Bobby asked the dreamtakers.

Zis gave him a tiny blue jewel. "This is blue moonstone and it gives off light in the dark."

"Thank you," said Bobby.

"Thank you," said Kat.

"Ditto," said Teabag.

The three children and the budgie went into the passage again and the darkness was replaced by a beautiful blue light, which was even more striking because of the greyness everywhere else.

Bobby whispered to Arnie. "Fly on ahead and try and see if you can find any booby traps, or guards."

Why don't you fly on ahead, you're the blinking Superhero?

"Because, I can't fly."

You're not much of a Superhero, are you?

Arnie darted off into the deep blue light, twittering on and on.

As Bobby crept through the passage, he admired the deep blue light and started to think of Caribbean oceans and azure skies, and whilst he was daydreaming he trod on an iron plate and three spears shot out from the shadows and flew just over his head and hit the opposite wall. Whap! Whap! Whap! He stood there, a little stunned, and realised these spears had probably been meant to kill an adult, and as he was a foot smaller than your average adult, the spears had flown just over his head.

Kat tutted and wagged her finger in front of Bobby's face. "You'd better pay more attention, mate, unless you want a head full of holes."

CHAPTER ELEVEN

THE MASTERS

The children reached the end of the passage and there was a ladder leading up to the dungeons. They climbed to the top of the ladder and clambered into the dungeons. All the separate prison cells were empty, but they felt a chill running up their spines when they noticed the cells were strewn with human bones. They tiptoed through the dungeons trying not to look at all the fleshless skulls, because their hollow eyes seemed to follow them wherever they went. They tiptoed to the dungeon door and tried the handle. The door was unlocked, and Bobby eased it open a couple of centimetres and peered into the corridor.

There were several guards marching up and down, wearing gold uniforms and large jewel encrusted helmets.

Bobby whispered to the other two. "Wait here until I come and get you."

"Good idea," said Teabag nodding his head.

"Shouldn't we all stick together?" asked Kat.

"It will be easier if I go on my own."

"Good idea," said Teabag nodding his head.

Bobby sneaked into the corridor and closed the dungeon door behind him. He rubbed his eyes and immediately disappeared. He dodged the guards and headed for the spiral staircase that led up to the highest rooms in the castle. He opened the door at the top of the stairs and entered a dark room where he could hear a low growling sound. He took the blue moonstone out of his pocket and it lit up the room. His face was a centimetre away from the biggest tiger he'd ever seen. He was so close, the tiger's breath was blowing his hair back as it breathed. He zipped back through the door and slammed it shut behind him as he didn't fancy reappearing in front of a hungry tiger. Then it dawned on him. The tiger had a couple of little green feathers around its mouth. The huge cat had obviously eaten his budgie. Bobby was totally devastated, but he had to complete his mission.

Whilst he was still invisible, he passed through rooms that contained lions, bears and alligators. One room even had a six headed rhinoceros inside, and he'd never seen one of those back in his own time. On his journey he triggered off rifles, crossbows, spears and flamethrowers. In the room where the flamethrowers were he found a small ruby lighter that someone had left behind and he put it in his pocket with the moonstone. As he left the room he became visible again. He would have to be even more vigilant now.

The Masters were in their room studying a giant computer screen on their gold plated wall. The computer was showing them images of all the weaponry being mysteriously triggered off, and their only clue was all the doors that were opening and closing as if by magic.

The six Masters were named in alphabetical order from A – F. Aba was the top Master, and then Bix, Coot, Dud, Egon and Fabb followed next. They were all dressed in long gold cloaks and had their hair dyed gold as well.

Aba raised her arms in the air and all the other Masters fell silent. "It seems as if our castle has a ghost."

Bix rose from the computer. "Our computers tell us there are three extra human heart beats in the castle. I don't think ghosts have heart beats, your Topness." As Bix was saying this a trap door opened in the corner of the room and two small children clambered out.

Kat and Teabag had found a ladder in the dungeon and they had decided to find out where it went. Now they knew.

The Masters pressed their ray guns up against the children's' heads.

Aba peered at her two captives. "Well, well, well, what have we here?"

"They must be the owners of the extra heart beats," Coot replied.

"But there are three extra heart beats," said Bix, "and there are only two children here."

"Then the missing heart beat must belong to the one who is setting off all our booby traps," Dud reasoned.

Aba ordered Egon and Fabb to chain the youngsters in two large metal chairs. Then Coot marched over and blindfolded them.

Only then did Aba approach the children. "You are now shackled to the Chairs of Death!" she cried in an overdramatic way.

Teabag shuddered. "I don't suppose you use these for watching telly then."

"It would be better for you if you tell us where your friend is," hissed Aba.

"We haven't got any friends," said Teabag.

"We only want the one who broke into the castle with you."

"Oh, we did that on our own," said Kat.

"Very well, I will give you a few seconds to see if your memory returns."

"What if it doesn't?" asked Teabag.

"Do you know what damage a ray gun does to a

human head?"

The children shook their heads.

"Then you will soon find out!" snapped Aba. "Unless you tell us what we want to know." She aimed the ray gun at one of the smaller computers and blew it to smithereens.

The children gulped out loud.

Bobby was closing in on the Masters' headquarters. He opened the door to another room and crept inside.

A deep booming voice rumbled. "Welcome to your death!"

The youngster turned to see a twelve foot Cyclops standing in front of him, and it was the fiercest creature he'd come across yet.

It was wearing dark red plates of armour and carrying a net in its right claw and a giant silver spear in its left.

Bobby didn't really know what to do, but he eventually said. "Oh, I'm sorry, I thought these were the toilets. I must have made a wrong turn back there, I'll be on my way then." He edged his way slowly back to the doorway. "Erm, nice suit of armour by the way, you look really good in red."

"There is no escape from the Cyclops," growled the giant.

"A Cyclops?" cried the worried boy. "But you don't exist."

The Cyclops roared with laughter. "I suppose we must be dreaming then. Have you ever had your lungs pulled up through your nostrils in a dream before?"

Bobby quivered. "No, I think I would have remembered that one."

The Cyclops pounced.

Bobby's heart almost jumped out of his chest. He'd never been this frightened in all his life.

As the Cyclops grabbed him round the throat and lifted its spear above its head...

Time came grinding to a halt.

The youngster let out a shaky laugh and sighed. "Perfect timing."

He prised the spear from the hand of the Cyclops and rammed it with all his might through its only eye, then he yanked it out again. He ran to the door at the far end of the room and the spear he carried left a trail of thick blood behind him. He pressed a golden button by the side of the door and it slid open with a whoosh. Inside the room he discovered the Masters in various frozen positions. He also noticed that Kat and Teabag were in the room, chained in giant silver chairs. He had enough time to run the spear through Bix, Coot, Dud, Egon and Fabb. Time started again as he aimed the spear at Aba's heart.

Aba was horrified to find herself confronted by this berserk little boy. She wasn't too bothered about her fellow Masters as they lay bleeding at her feet, but this boy was now threatening her life, and that was an entirely different matter.

Kat and Teabag sat quietly in the corner of the room wondering what was happening.

Aba regarded the youngster with disdain. "Do you know who I am?"

"Yes, you're one of the Masters."

"That is right, boy, I am top Master and I am your leader!" Then she pointed an accusing finger at him. "You have committed treason by killing the others and you should be executed, but I will pardon you if you surrender to me now."

"I'm sorry," countered Bobby, "but you have changed the world into a horrible grey place, you have murdered millions of your own people, and stolen the dreams of the rest." He paused for a few seconds as he felt he had forgotten something. "Oh yes...and you've also killed my budgie. *You're* the one who must surrender."

Aba whipped a ray gun from her belt and laughed an evil laugh. "Are you ready to surrender now?" She pointed the ray gun at his head.

Bobby had seen Aba reaching for her gun and he had taken the ruby lighter out of his pocket and flicked back the top and lit the flame.

The top ranking Master seemed very puzzled by this, and then she let out a terrific laugh. "What are you going to do with that, singe me to death?"

They stood there like two gunfighters from a cowboy movie. All that was missing was the gunfight music. They stared deep into each others' eyes, beads of sweat forming on their brows.

Aba suddenly lifted the ray gun and pressed the trigger.

As she did this Bobby breathed hard on the lighter's flame. The ray from the gun flashed by his head, but he had been much more accurate and the Master was burnt to a cinder. The gunslinger blew out the lighter's flame and put it back in his pocket. He had the fastest ruby lighter in the west.

Arnie fluttered over and landed on one of the Masters great computers. He stared down at the billowing remains of the top Master.

I thought your Chemistry teacher had warned you about playing with fire.

"Boy, am I glad to see you!" cried Bobby running over to the budgie. "I thought you'd been eaten by the tiger."

That little pussycat? I don't think so.

"But I saw green feathers around its mouth. How did you escape?"

I punched it on the nose.

"You punched a tiger on the nose?"

I flew into the tiger in the dark, it tried to eat me, so I belted it and scarpered, double quick.

"Excuse me," Teabag called out from the other side of the room. "Could anyone tell me what is going on?"

"Flipping heck, I'd forgotten all about those two." Bobby ran over to the Chairs of Death and unchained his two companions.

Kat and Teabag tore off their blindfolds and squinted at him.

Kat stared around the room in astonishment. "You've killed all the Masters. They all had mega ray guns. How on earth did you manage that?"

Bobby made a few chopping movements with his hands. "I've been taking Kung Fu lessons." He stopped slicing the air with his hand. "But how did you get here before me?"

Kat pointed at the ladder which led to the dungeon. "We climbed up that."

"A ladder from the dungeon!" groaned Bobby slapping himself on the head. "I would have saved myself a load of hassle if I'd known about the ladder." Then he led them back into the room where the Cyclops lay dead.

Teabag stood beside the dead monster. "What the hell is that?"

"It's a Cyclops."

"You killed a Cyclops with Kung Fu?"

"Yes, but it did take me a couple of minutes."

The children concentrated on escaping from the castle, but they couldn't go back through the castle because of all the wild animals and guards, and so they took the net from the hand of the Cyclops and tore it into strands. Then they tied the rope strands to the window and climbed down the castle wall. They skirted around the castle until they met up with Zis and Zat.

After the dreamtakers had been told of the Masters' demise, they explained how the guards would disband without their leaders, and Upper England could be returned to the people.

Zis and Zat thanked the children. "We will get the scientists to restore our dreams and we will tear up the concrete and plant trees. The future will be more like the past." They thanked the children once again and then they used their crystals to open the worm-hole for the very last time.

Bobby, Arnie, Kat and Teabag stepped into the worm-hole and were whirred back into the past.

After they stepped back out from the worm-hole they stood and watched in silence as the doorway to the future shrank and disappeared.

Arnie bounced up and down on Bobby's head.

I never thought I'd be so glad to see some trees. I'll see you when you get home.

The budgie took to the sky and soared over the trees and out of sight.

Bobby was thinking how it would have been nice to have been given some flying powers, and, as he was thinking this, he heard someone running through the bushes.

This someone sprang out of the bushes and came to a standstill right in front of him.

What Bobby saw next shook him so much that his hair stood on end. For standing right in front of Bobby Coleman was... Bobby Coleman. It was as if he were staring into a mirror. So he said to this other Bobby. "What are you doing here?"

"Escaping from the Shadow."

In a flash the young Superhero realised the dreamtakers had sent them back a day earlier than they were supposed to, so he said to the other Bobby. "All I can tell you is this, I've just been sent back from your future a day earlier than I should have been. You're going to have a great adventure tomorrow night, but it is vital that you tell Zis and Zat to be more careful when they send you back."

"Okay, thanks," said the other Bobby. And he ran off shouting, "I'd better get going! I'm late for my supper!"

"Did that really happen?" asked a bewildered Teabag.

"This time travelling lark is more complicated than it looks," said Kat.

Bobby wondered what would happen to them now, because they weren't supposed to be in this time. They were out of place. He didn't have to wait long to find out, because the three children gradually faded away to nothing. The reason they faded away was because nature has a way of putting things back in order.

Not too far away, a little green budgie that was soaring through the clouds, also faded away to nothing.

On Wednesday morning Bobby awoke and the first thing he did was write on a piece of paper:

Tell Zis and Zat to be more careful sending us back.

Then he lived through the same events as he had previously done, until twelve hours later, he and his friends were sent back by Zis and Zat and arrived home exactly when they were supposed to.

Bobby was the *only* Bobby Coleman once again, and he was *very* relieved as it can be quite disturbing meeting yourself.

CHAPTER TWELVE

PIRANHA FOOD

That night Bobby decided to stay in and watch telly as he was worn out and needed to recharge his Superhero batteries.

He was sat on the yellow leather couch in the living room, with his mum and little Anna squeezed in next to him.

Mr Coleman lounged in his matching yellow armchair with Sparky lay across his lap and Arnie perched on Sparky's head.

The family were ready for some serious television viewing, and there was nothing more serious than their favourite soap opera, Geezers. This week they tuned in to find out whether their favourite geezer Frank the Tank had escaped from the burning offices that his mother-in-law had set on fire by accident whilst arguing with Frank the Tank's boss who was blackmailing her over the adopted boy that she had raised who had been caught stealing from the office safe disguised as a policewoman – or something like that. As the family sat in suspense, Frank the Tank pulled a gun on his boss and was just about to shoot him and... the telly went on the blink.

The whole Coleman family were up in arms.

Mr Coleman jumped up and attacked the telly, sending Sparky and Arnie sprawling across the room. He was beating it with his fists and when this didn't work he gave it a mighty kick. As this had no effect he threatened the television with death, which was quite entertaining for the rest of the family.

"You." Thump, "stupid." Thump, "blinking." Thump, "pile." Thump, "of junk." Thump. Kick. Thump, "I'll kill you!"

Anna looked up to the heavens in despair. "Beating up the telly isn't going to make it work, dad."

"I know petal, it just makes me feel better." Thump. Thump. Kick.

Then the picture began to clear and Anna told her dad to get out of the way.

Mr Coleman jumped back in his armchair, but it wasn't Frank the Tank that appeared on the screen.

Instead it was a young teenager dressed from head to toe in black. This is what he had to say. "People of the World, do not adjust your set, as I am on every television on the planet." He popped a few flies in his mouth. "I am the Shadow, and I am soon to be the ruler of this planet. I am here to introduce myself to my future subjects. I plan to take over the world at seven 'o'clock tonight, and those who do not comply to my wishes will simply have to die. Oh, and before I forget, I have a personal message to a very good friend of mine. I have a couple of your friends with me and if you do not join me soon, they will be swimming with the piranhas. Yum, yum," and the Shadow licked his lips and rubbed his tummy as his image slowly faded into the ether.

"Is that some kind of new game show?" asked Mrs Coleman.

Mr Coleman pulled a face. "Don't be silly. That was the new Channel Five newsreader."

Mrs Coleman peered down her nose at her husband. "Since when do newsreaders eat flies?"

But Bobby knew who it was. And he knew who the

Shadow was holding captive.

Inside the castle, Kat and Teabag were tied together on a narrow plank that was suspended over the piranha tank.

To take his mind off the vicious fish circling below, Teabag glanced down at the Shadow and said. "Why are you so interested in Bobby Coleman?"

The Shadow continued to type at his computer. "He has skills that I may find useful when I am ruling the world."

Kat seemed a little puzzled. "The only skills he has are whistling through his fingers and burping the national anthem."

The Shadow clattered relentlessly on his keyboard. "Then you do not know your friend very well."

"What do you mean?"

"Look, will you please be quiet!" snapped the Shadow. "I'm trying to take over the world here, and it would be a lot easier if you two weren't blabbering on."

"How on earth are you going to rule the world?" said Kat. "You're not much older than we are."

The Shadow straightened his back and sighed. "It is a grave mistake to underestimate me. That is why you are hanging above a tank of ravenous fish, and I am not."

"You haven't got the guts to drop us in the tank," Teabag said without any real conviction.

The Shadow glared at Teabag. "If you don't shut your trap, those piranhas won't be hungry for much longer!" Then he walked to the piranha tank and put his hand in the water and swirled it around. The piranhas swam for his fingers like crazy underwater rockets and at the very last moment he pulled out his hand and let out a mad little giggle. "Just a small demonstration."

"You're a flipping nutcase," said Kat.

"Maybe I am, but at least I'm not fish food." And the Shadow swept out of the room, and then he swept back in again because he had forgotten his keys. He looked a little embarrassed as he swept back out of the room again.

Teabag peered down at the fish. "Those piranhas look very hungry."

"Will you stop talking about the piranhas," rapped Kat.

"Well, what else is there to talk about when you're suspended four foot over a tank full of starving killer fish? Perhaps, you'd like to discuss the weather?"

"At least it would take our minds off being eaten alive." The young girl tried to change the subject. "I think the Shadow is a real loner, don't you?"

"How do you make that out?"

"He has all the classic symptoms. Especially wanting to rule the world. I mean, fancy calling yourself the Shadow, I bet his real name is something like Tarquin."

"Good point," said Teabag. "I just happen to think he's bananas."

"See, you can put the piranhas out of your mind when you try."

"Yes, I was doing alright," agreed Teabag nodding his head, "until you mentioned the pigging things again."

"If you don't quit moaning," hissed Kat, "I'll feed you to the flipping piranhas myself."

Bobby was using the blue moonstone to find his way through the passage that Zis and Zat had shown him in the future.

Unfortunately, Arnie couldn't be with him tonight as he was spring cleaning his cage. What's more important, Bobby had asked him, saving the world or spring cleaning

90

your cage? He had been surprised to hear such language from a budgie. So tonight he was on his own.

"At least I know the castle like the back of my hand," Bobby said quietly, as he fell into a deep pit. After he had climbed out of the pit, he dusted himself down and reminded himself not to be so cocky.

Fifteen minutes later, Bobby entered the chamber that led to the Shadow's main living quarters, and he noticed that there was now a giant golden throne in the room.

The Shadow was sat upon the throne.

Bobby approached the throne. "This boy has got *serious* identity problems."

"I see that we meet again, Coleman."

"Why do you keep talking like that? That's not the way normal people talk."

The Shadow drummed his fingers on the arms of the throne. "We are not normal people, Coleman. We are blessed with Superpowers." He drifted off deep into thought. After a moment or two he opened his eyes wide. "If you don't help me rule the world I will turn your friends into piranha food."

Bobby crossed his fingers behind his back. "Okay, I agree. Let my friends go and then you can tell me all your plans."

"At last you have come to your senses," purred a delighted Shadow. "You will grow accustomed to being evil, it gets easier once you have done one or two terrible things. Now I will tell you my plans as I know you will never break your Superhero word."

Bobby had crossed his fingers when he had agreed to help the Shadow, and that meant all promises were null and void.

"This is my evil plan," the Shadow began. "I'm not sure if I've told you all my Superpowers, but the one I'm most proud of is my hypnotic power..."

"It beats eating flies I suppose," Bobby whispered under his breath.

"...and as I have control over all the televisions on the planet, tonight I shall hypnotise the world and they shall be forever in my power. Pretty nifty, eh."

"What about the people who don't watch television?"

"Everyone watches television!" barked the Shadow. "But your job will be to organise the deaths of anyone who somehow misses my performance. It's a very, very ingenious plan, even if I do say so myself.".

"It is a very clever plan, Shadow," said Bobby, buttering him up. "I will be honoured to help you as soon as you let my friends go."

"If you were really evil, you would feed them to the piranhas yourself."

"I'm only a beginner, Shadow. You can't expect me to be as evil as you without any practise."

"Evil is as evil does," said the Shadow.

"Pardon?" said Bobby.

The Shadow ignored Bobby and sighed. "Go ahead then, let them go. I am in a merciful mood. I will feed the piranhas a few of my ex-school friends when they are in my power. The Shadow is tired now and must rest before tonight's broadcast. Waken me at seven 'o'clock, Coleman." The Shadow swept out of the room, then he swept back in, picked up his keys, kicked his throne in frustration, and swept back out again.

Bobby went through to where his friends were dangling over a tank full of piranhas. He walked over to them and stared through the glass tank. "These fish really do have very sharp little teeth, don't they? Quite vicious looking really, and to think there's only that thin piece of rope between you and the most horrible death you can imagine."

"Please, Bobby," implored Teabag, "this is not the time to start being funny."

"Are you suggesting that I wasn't funny before." teased Bobby.

"No, he wasn't," said Kat. "We both know you're a comic genius. Now please get us down before the rope snaps."

The young Superhero swung the plank away from the piranha tank and lowered it to the floor, then he untied his friends.

"Eat this!" cried Teabag, sticking his tongue out at the piranhas.

"Wait until I get my hand on our Shadowy friend," snarled Kat. "I'm going to introduce him to his piranhas!"

Bobby explained what was happening and he told them of his plan to end the Shadow's reign of terror before it even got started.

The three children were working as fast as they could as they only had until seven 'o'clock to get everything exactly right. The world depended on it.

At seven 'o'clock Bobby woke the Shadow.

The Shadow yawned and told him he would join him in the computer room after he had showered and changed.

Half an hour later, the Shadow swept into the room, and they prepared for the television transmission that would change the world.

The Shadow used all his mathematical and computer genius to control the world's satellites. It was time to tap into all the televisions on the planet once again. All over the world, on televisions far and wide, on televisions big and small, on televisions loud and quiet, the Shadow slowly came into view. Once he had used his hypnotic powers they would all be like putty in his hand. It didn't even matter whether people understood English or not, as it was his Shadowy eyes that would hypnotise them all.

The Shadow turned to the children and clapped his hands. "Let the show begin."

Moments later, the whole world were watching the Shadow once more. He blinked his dark eyes. "Greetings to the world. Today is the dawn of a new era. You will soon feel the force of the Shadow's power, but first you must look deep into my eyes, deeper, deeper..."

As the television watching audience began to feel sleepy, Teabag threw a lever that he and his friends had rigged up while the Shadow was asleep. The lever released a giant mirror that dropped between the Shadow and the cameras.

Bobby and Kat held the Shadow down, and he was forced to stare at his own reflection.

The Shadow let out a loud scream as he stared into his own dark hypnotic eyes and moments later he was in a deep, deep trance.

Teabag switched off the transmitter and all the world went back to their football, quiz shows and soap operas, and they would never hear from the Shadow again.

While the Shadow was in a trance, Bobby knelt down and put his mouth right up to his ear and whispered. "You are not the Shadow. The Shadow is dead. You are Tarquin McWhacker. You have no Superpowers and you will have no memory of having any. You are a rich young man, who will spend the rest of his life using his wealth to bring some good to the world."

He clicked his fingers and the Shadow was gone forever.

And in his place awoke the new and improved Tarquin McWhacker. He shook all the cobwebs out of his mind. "Where am I?"

"Hello, Tarquin," said Bobby. "You're at home, and you've had a little bump on the head and lost your memory, but I'll tell you exactly what you need to know."

After he had told Tarquin who he was and what he was to do, they said their goodbyes, and Tarquin never did anything but good from that day on.

As they were leaving the castle, Kat said to the boys. "No wonder he went mad, I mean, fancy being called Tarquin McWhacker."

CHAPTER THIRTEEN

MORATH THE DEMON

The American Superheroes had become too famous and this is why they were no longer saving the world. Everybody knew who they were and all about their strengths and weaknesses. They made the best of their lives by appearing in adverts and guesting on talk shows, because they were all celebrities now. If the planet was in immediate danger from some evil force or another, then there was no point expecting one of the American Superheroes to save you, because they just weren't up to the job anymore.

When Bobby was thwarting the invasion of the Minkys all the truly great American Superheroes were attending the movie premiere of the latest Batman film. Nobody even knew there was a Superhero in England and this is why Bobby is the busiest on the planet.

But life settled down to some kind of normality over the next few months. Bobby finished the school year in the top half of his class, and second from bottom in Maths. In late July he celebrated his thirteenth birthday. The uneventful warm summer months were to lull him into a false sense of security. Perhaps he wouldn't be needing his Superpowers anymore. Perhaps he could hang up his Superboots and retire.

September signalled the beginning of another school year.

October brought the most frightening adventure that our Superhero had been on yet for trouble was brewing, and it was brewing right underneath Witches Woods.

Imprisoned in a cavern beneath the woods was a demon called Morath. He had been imprisoned over ten thousand years ago, for incurring the wrath of the four most powerful demons of the time – Khar, Vendor, Reeva and Heckaty. Morath's crime was to flay alive some innocent people without their permission, and for that he was to be imprisoned under ground for eternity.

At first, the demons were so angry they were going to imprison him in total darkness, but Morath pleaded for them to be merciful and allow him to have a light to read by, because he was an expert on demonic literature and loved to read.

After the demons had calmed down, they decided that as Morath was a fellow demon, they would place an eternal flame in the cavern and allow him to take all the demon literature he wanted.

So Morath had spent the last ten thousand years reading such devilish books as: "The Sound of Darkness;" "Essential Evil and How to Get It;" and, "Flaying People Alive – How to Get the Most From Your Whips." All the books were bound in the skin of dragons and written in the blood of unicorns, and this is why there are no dragons and unicorns alive today.

Morath now possessed the greatest knowledge of any demon this side of the universe and he had no more use for his demonic books. It had taken him ten thousand years to discover all their secrets and now all he could think of was escape and revenge.

Morath had spent the last hundred years devising his plans. The cavern was meant to be escape proof, but he had other ideas. Soon he would make the other demons pay. He would make human kind pay as well. They had done nothing to him, but he'd been seething with rage for over ten thousand years, and the whole puny planet was going to know about it.

Morath knew how to escape and he knew exactly who to recruit to help him wage his war. And is there a better time for a demon to set his evil plans to work than Halloween?

Tonight it was Halloween, and Bobby planned to go trick or treating with Kat and Teabag. They met at six 'o'clock outside his house, and they were all kitted out in fancy dress. Bobby was in a skeleton suit, Kat was made up as a vampire, and Teabag had a white sheet over his head, because his mum wouldn't buy him a costume as she thought Halloween was a waste of time.

The night went very well and they all had bags bursting with treats.

Then Teabag suddenly said. "I dare you to go into Witches Woods."

"Don't be stupid, Teabag," chided Kat. "Nobody goes in there after dark, and especially not on Halloween."

"Do I hear the sound of a chicken clucking?" taunted Teabag.

Kat tutted. "No, you hear the sound of a sensible person deciding not to do something totally daft."

"Cluck cluck cluck," clucked Teabag.

Kat was becoming a little annoyed. "Grow up, Teabag."

"Hey, we're teenagers now," said Teabag. "Why don't we start acting like teenagers? We should be brave and bold and fearless. I could always hold your hand, Kat."

Saying that to Kat was like holding up a red rag in front of a bull. She snorted and fumed. "Okay, melon head, let's get going."

"Come on you two," said Bobby, "let's have a reality check here. Teabag, this is not one of your greatest ideas."

"Oh listen, more chickens," laughed Teabag. "We must have walked into a farmyard."

Even though Bobby was a Superhero, he was also a young teenager, and he wasn't letting Teabag get away with that. "Lead on then braveheart, let's see what Witches Woods holds in store for us."

A chilly shiver ran up their spines.

Below the ground, Morath was chanting an ancient spell. He held the eternal flame in the palm of his hand and after hours of repeating the incantation the flame swirled faster and faster, and when he finished speaking and opened his eyes, the deep red flame rose to the cavern ceiling and began to burn through the rock.

A few hours later, Morath bore witness to the sky for the first time in ten thousand years. And it felt good. He was ready to make this world pay for ten thousand years of captivity and his revenge would be swift and terrible. But first he had four demons to sort out.

The three children were in the woods.

Teabag was nervously scanning his surroundings. "Does anyone get the feeling we are being watched?"

"Someone is *definitely* watching you," Kat replied.

"Who?" Teabag cried in panic.

"*Me*, stupid," giggled Kat.

"Yes, very funny, Kat. Aren't you afraid of anything?"

"No."

Teabag shook his white sheet. "Not even the ghost of the old station master. Whoooo!"

"You might think this is funny," said Kat, "but we're

acting like all those stupid kids in the movies. The ones that go into the dark, dark woods even when there's some kind of monster prowling around."

"That's right," agreed Bobby. "You sit there watching them, thinking how daft they are, and then they all get eaten and everyone cheers the monster."

Kat nodded solemnly. "Well, we're turning into those stupid kids."

"Who said anything about monsters?" said Teabag.

There was a loud howling noise from deep within the woods.

Bobby gulped. "Okay, we've all shown how brave we are. I'm turning back before we get lost?"

"Sounds good to me," said Kat, "You can go on alone, Teabag, we don't mind."

"No, it's okay, fellow chickens, I'll be heading back with you."

The youngsters heard someone rushing through the bushes, and they stood frozen to the spot as a small creature passed them by.

The creature was three foot high and was bright red, it had long red hair and two horns directly above its pointed ears. The top half of the creature was human-like, but the bottom half resembled a goat. The creature was wearing silvery blue armour. The creature was Morath. He was the smallest demon in the universe, but he made up for this by being the most vicious. However, he was too wrapped up in his own wrath to notice the children.

Teabag glanced at the others. "That has got to be the *worst* Halloween costume I've ever seen."

Bobby was not so sure. What would such a small kid be doing alone in Witches Woods at this time of night? He decided it would be a good idea to find out where this small person was off to. "I'm going to follow him, he might be lost."

Morath knew exactly where he wanted to go, and he went there as fast as his little hairy legs would carry him. He reached Milltown cemetery and swung open the large wrought iron gates and marched into the heart of the graveyard.

The children were following close behind.

Teabag whispered. "Out of the frying pan into the fire."

"What is this little kid up to?" said Kat. "Has he got some kind of death wish?"

Teabag shrugged. "Perhaps he just likes danger."

Bobby was concentrating on keeping the little red figure in sight, but it was difficult, because the graveyard was only dimly lit, and the further they ventured in, the darker it got. Eventually he lost sight of the little red figure and swung round to the other two. "Did anyone see where he went?"

"No," said Teabag, "but I think we should disappear too. It's getting dark in here and this is even spookier than the woods." He turned and stared at the giggling Kat. "What's the matter with you?"

"You're wandering around Milltown cemetery dressed as a ghost."

"You think that's funny, do you?"

"Hilarious," she blurted out as she broke down with laughter.

"Shut up will you," barked Bobby. "You're making enough noise to waken the dead."

"What did you go and say that for?" Teabag said with a shudder.

CHAPTER FOURTEEN

SKELETONS

Morath had disappeared into an old tomb. He was ready for his revenge. He held his little red hands in the air and called upon the wind:

"North wind send your wrath to me,
Make my enemies appear,
The ones that caught and banished me,
Blow those demons here."

The wind began to stir and the wind began to rage and less than a moment later the four demons were blown into the tomb.

Khar, Vendor, Reeva and Heckaty were incensed at being summoned like this. They were even more incensed, because they were about to indulge in their favourite pastime, which was skinning people alive and dipping them in salt.

Khar spoke first in deep demonic tones. "We are most surprised to see you again Morath. Where have you been for the last ten thousand years?"

The demons cackled with laughter.

Morath eyed the demons with scorn. "You may as well laugh now, because where I'm going to send you is no laughing matter."

"Oh dear," mocked Vendor, "the little red demon is threatening us. Hey lads, I'm shaking with fear."

The demons started cackling again.

Morath whispered a quick incantation. "Maybe this will shut you up."

The four demons moved menacingly towards him.

Khar spoke again. "We grow tired of your pathetic threats Morath, it is time we sent you below again, and this time, no books." As soon as he said this there was a flash of blue light and the four demons found they could not move.

"What kind of trickery is this?" Reeva demanded to know.

"Oh, it's just a little magic," taunted Morath. "It's surprising what tricks you can pick up in ten thousand years."

"Release us!" boomed Heckaty. "Or we will tear you into a million pieces."

"Now, now, Heckaty, I don't think you're really in a position to be making threats. I have waited a long time for this moment and soon I will be rid of you forever and then I shall conquer this puny planet."

"Come, Morath," Khar said in a sly voice. "Let us not be hasty. We have misjudged you and we are willing to let you return to the demon family. Undo your spell."

"You certainly have misjudged me," confirmed Morath. "You do so again if you think I will free you. It is your turn to find out what ten thousand years entombed in the earth is like, but unlike me you will have no eternal flame to give you light." Morath chanted a touch more magic.

For the first time in their lives the four ancient demons tasted fear.

Vendor seethed. "Let us go, you little red squirt, because if you don't we are going to make you very, very sorry."

"Oh, I don't think so. Now *please* show some manners while I cast my spell." Morath began waving his arms as if he was conducting an orchestra:

"To molten fire beneath the earth,
I summon you from deep deep down,
Burn your way through rocks and earth,
And drag these demons underground."

There rose from the earth a deep gurgling sound and a loud grinding noise, and then, with a terrible earth shattering crash, the ground below the demons was torn asunder. There was a surge of blood red smoke from within this fissure, and the four demons sank screaming into the ground. When they were gone the earth slowly closed up again and all was silent once more.

Morath's face was contorted by wickedness. "Say hello to the worms for me."

It was time for the demon to conquer the world. For that he needed an army and he knew exactly where to find one.

The children were ready to call off the search when they heard the sound of the earth quaking.

Teabag jumped and scanned the graveyard. "That is *just* the sort of noise that I *don't* want to hear when I'm stood in the middle of a cemetery on Halloween."

Bobby stared down at the ground. "It sounded like an earthquake."

"Milltown isn't exactly famed for its earthquakes though, is it?" reasoned Kat.

Bobby pointed to the centre of the graveyard. "It came from over that way."

Teabag pointed in the opposite direction. "Then I

think we should go this way."

"The little boy might be in trouble," said Bobby.

"We might be in trouble too, if we go where that sound came from," argued Teabag.

"Come on, Teabag," said Kat, "we can't leave him out here alone."

So the skeleton, the vampire and the ghost ran towards the place where the noise had come from.

Morath was outside the tomb and he was whispering a very powerful incantation. One it had taken him thousands of years to unearth and understand. It was an incantation of the dead. Morath wanted an army. An army of skeletons. But only the skeletons of wicked people could be raised. He thought there would be enough evil skeletons in a graveyard as big as Milltowns to raise a decent army, and so he whispered away:

"To evil skulls and evil bones,
To evil left and evil right,
To skeletons beneath the ground,
Arise for me tonight."

A deep cold wind howled and purple and blue clouds gathered above the graveyard. Then, with a terrible ferocity, purple bolts of lightning struck down and split certain gravestones in half.

The children were wondering why Milltown's weather had gone totally barmy, and while they stood with puzzled faces, a skeletal hand pushed up through the earth and grabbed Teabag's ankle.

Teabag faced the other two and gulped. "Please tell me that I'm only imagining that something has got hold of my leg."

Kat glanced down. "It's okay, Teabag, you're not imagining it."

"What is it then?"

"Looks like the hand of a skeleton."

The children thought about this for a micro second, then they screamed and ran out through the cemetery gates at close to the speed of sound.

An elderly couple across the road were on their way home from a local restaurant, and the old man looked at his wife. "I've just seen a ghost running out of Milltown cemetery."

"Don't be a silly old fool," said his wife. "You've been drinking too much wine again."

"I better not mention the vampire and the skeleton," he muttered under his breath.

CHAPTER FIFTEEN

COTTONFORD

As the youngsters were racing home faster than the wind, Bobby suddenly skidded to a halt and slowly walked back to the cemetery. Of course, he didn't want to. Who would? But a Superhero's gotta do, what a Superhero's gotta do.

Teabag grabbed hold of Bobby's arm. "Where do you think you're going?"

"Someone's got to save that kid."

"Are you crazy!" cried Teabag. "Any kid who goes alone into a graveyard on Halloween after dark deserves to be set on by skeletons."

Bobby stared into his friend's eyes. "You don't really mean that."

"Oh, don't I?" challenged Teabag.

"Okay, Teabag," said Bobby shaking his arm free, "I'm not knocking you for leaving, but me and Kat are going back."

Bobby and Kat set off for the cemetery.

After a short distance Teabag caught them up. "If I get torn to pieces by skeletons, you can explain it to my mum and dad."

The thought of skeletons frightened Bobby more than anything else in the world, but he knew the little red creature must have something to do with all this, and it was his duty, as a Superhero, to find out what that was.

Once inside the cemetery they saw skeleton after skeleton climbing up from their graves and shaking the soil from their bones.

As Bobby was dressed up as a skeleton he blended in well, and he told the other two to stay close behind him for cover.

In the centre of Milltown cemetery was a large tomb, where the richest family in the town had been buried for centuries, and the skeletons were all marching inside.

Morath was inside the tomb, and it was brightly lit by the eternal flame.

In this bright bright light, the children could clearly see the little red creature they'd been following was some kind of demon.

The demon spoke. "I am Morath the most powerful demon on the face of the planet, and after ten thousand years of imprisonment I intend to make this world my own. I have summoned you here to be part of my army. You are the skeletons of the evil and you will serve me well. Every night we will march on a new cemetery and recruit more skeletons. Every night we will go underground, until one day our army is big enough to wage war on the world. Any skeleton not evil enough to do this, should climb back into their grave right now."

All the skeletons remained where they were.

"Good!" hissed the demon. "Tonight we march on Cottonford cemetery."

Morath and the skeleton army marched for three miles until they reached Cottonford cemetery, and the children weren't too far behind.

The strange red demon conjured up the Cottonford skeletons. This time he was hoping for a few more skeletons than he got in Milltown, which obviously wasn't a very evil place. The storm clouds soon gathered again and the supernatural purple lightning began to strike the earth.

One of the skeletons beside Bobby suddenly spoke. "He's very good, isn't he? I hear he's one of the more evil demons around, and he has some terrible rage problems that he needs to resolve."

"How will he resolve them?" asked Bobby, not really wanting to hear the answer.

"By slaughtering humans, I should imagine."

Bobby swallowed hard and wondered what he had let himself in for.

The skeleton stared at him with its big empty eye sockets.

This was really beginning to freak Bobby out.

Then the skeleton spoke again. "Hang on a minute, you're not a real skeleton, you're just wearing a skeleton suit."

"I am a skeleton," protested Bobby. "I'm only wearing this because I'm cold."

"Liar!" shrieked the skeleton. "Skeletons can't feel the cold, and who's that cowering behind you? Morath! Morath! We have intruders in our midst!"

All the gathered Milltown and Cottonford skeletons stood and stared, causing the children's' knees to knock extremely loudly. The skeletons parted and Morath glided between them.

Morath glowered at Bobby. "Why are you dressed as a skeleton, human?"

"Don't you mean, why am I dressed as a human skeleton?"

"Why are you dressed as a skeleton?" Morath repeated with a touch more menace.

"Because I'm not dressed as a vampire."

"Are you trying to be amusing?"

"I can't help it, I'm an incredibly funny person."

"You are a very brave little human," said the demon.

Then he waved his hand and shrieked. "Kill them!"

The skeletons screeched out a war cry and rattled towards them.

Bobby had more control over his Superpowers than ever before and he ran through the graveyard with Kat and Teabag close behind. When they reached a giant tomb in the middle of the graveyard he screeched to a halt and shouted. "Quick, you two, hide behind that gravestone!"

As Bobby seemed to know what he was doing, the two children did as they were told.

They ducked down behind the headstone.

Kat whispered. "I thought Cottonford was supposed to be a boring town."

Bobby swung open the gate at the entrance of the tomb and dropped the blue moonstone so that it lit up the whole interior. He sprinted to the back of the tomb and waited until all the skeletons had followed him inside.

The skeletons crept silently towards him and he could feel evil in the air. This was more terrifying than all the Trolls, aliens and robots rolled into one. The nearest skeleton lunged for his throat.

Bobby quickly rubbed his eyes and vanished. He dodged by the skeletons and returned to the tomb entrance where he picked up the moonstone and put it back in his pocket. Then he took out the ruby lighter and flicked it open. At that moment he became visible again.

The skeletons saw him and crept towards him, but they were too late.

Bobby lit the lighter's flame and blew on it as hard as he could. The inside of the tomb lit up like an inferno and the skeletons were burnt to dust. Bobby whispered. "First you were buried and now you've been cremated, perhaps this time you'll rest in peace."

Kat peeped over the gravestone. "What happened in

there?"

Bobby gave a little shrug of the shoulders. "It just went up in flames."

Teabag stopped crouching behind the gravestone and stood up. "Lucky you weren't inside. It's like a red hot furnace in there."

"Yes, I suppose I was born lucky."

A voice from behind them squealed. "Your luck has just run out!"

The children spun round to see a breathtakingly horrible sight.

Morath was heading right for them, and he was breathing out flames of anger, and dark red smoke was billowing out of his ears. His little red hooves were causing sparks to fly off the graveyard path as he stormed towards them.

The children were petrified, but this still didn't stop Kat saying. "You'll give yourself indigestion, if you don't learn to relax."

The demon was so incredibly angry at this he threw a tantrum. He jumped up and down and pulled out tufts of red hair. Sparks from his hooves were flying everywhere and the top of his ears had set on fire as he snorted red steam and bellowed. "I loathe you! I loathe you! I loathe you with every fibre of my demon body! I loathe you so much that after you are dead I'm going to torture every single human on the planet, and it will all be *your* fault!"

Morath jumped up and grabbed Bobby by the throat. The demon's hands singed into the youngster's neck and he bared his fangs and laughed so loud that all the gravestones shook. He was about to tear out the teenager's throat when...

Time came screeching to a halt.

Bobby's heart was beating ten to the dozen and he

sighed with relief as he shook himself loose. But what could he do with this demon? If he didn't think of something quick, the whole human race was in for a big surprise.

He tried to frazzle the demon using his ruby lighter, but this had no effect at all.

Then he noticed a piece of paper poking out from the demon's armour and he pulled it free. It was an old piece of parchment that had gone brown with age, and it seemed to be written in blood. At the top of the paper it said, The Banishment Spell. Written below were the words of a magic incantation. Bobby read out the spell because he had nothing to lose by doing so:

"To where the sunlight never goes,
To caverns where it never snows,
Listen as I say these words,
I banish you beneath the earth."

As he was finishing the spell, time began again.

Morath awoke to hear the end of the incantation, and his face contorted in horror as he screamed. "You fool, what have you done..." There was a flash of blinding white light and Morath was gone.

Bobby didn't know what he'd done, but he was very glad he'd done it.

Kat and Teabag spoke at the same time. "Where did he go?"

"Back where he belongs," was Bobby's simple reply.

This year Halloween had certainly lived up to its name. The children left Cottonford cemetery and slowly wound their way home.

"I've lost my bag of treats," complained Teabag.

"Don't you ever stop thinking about your stomach?"

112

asked Kat.

"I had Mars bars, Snickers, Curly Wurlys and everything in that bag."

Up in the branches of the trees, the Cottonford birds applauded the children out of town. A large crow nudged his friend and squawked. "They must be the three children all the Milltown birds are raving on about."

His friend nodded and cawed. "It will be a long time before we see anything like that again. But we better get some sleep now, we've got to get up at dawn."

Deep underground, Morath reappeared in a cavern far far deeper than the one he had escaped from. It was pitch black in this cavern. But Morath thought he could hear the sound of somebody breathing, and so he said in a frightened little voice. "Is there anybody else down here?"

"*Yes*, there is," snarled four *very* angry demons.

CHAPTER SIXTEEN

THE FIGURE

Bobby watched helplessly as the Figure attacked Kat and Teabag, ripped out their hearts and threw them on the blazing red fire. He knew it had been a mistake to explore the old haunted railway station and now his best friends were dead.

The Figure moved slowly towards him and wrapped its long thin fingers around his neck and pulled him to its hooded face. Its features were hidden by shadows, but he could still feel its icy cold breath brushing his face, and his heart was racing as it lifted him above its head and launched him through the railway station window.

He was sent hurtling with a thousand shards of glass to the abandoned railway track below. As he fell he could hear someone in the distance crying. "Bobby, Bobby, Bobby." He opened his eyes to a beautiful blue light. "This must be heaven." And heaven looked a lot like, well, his bedroom. He was a little disappointed to say the least.

Bobby, Bobby, are you awake?

He shook the sleep from his mind and noticed Arnie perched on the rail at the bottom of his bed, with the blue moonstone held in his claws.

You were having a nightmare. You were screaming. "Save them from the Figure!"

Bobby slowly found his bearings. "That was the worst nightmare I've ever had, it felt so real. That's the last time I watch a vampire movie before I go to bed."

What did the Figure look like?

"You don't want to know, Arnie."

Yes *I do, that's why I'm asking.*

Bobby closed his eyes and forced himself to remember. "Well, it was wearing a dark cloak and it wore a hood that hid its face. I could see that it had terrible violet eyes and I could feel that it had freezing cold breath." A shiver ran right through his heart. "I don't really want to think about it anymore, Arnie."

There's an old bird legend that describes a Figure like the one you've just mentioned.

"What happens in the legend?"

The Figure's appearance signals the end of the world.

Bobby's eyes widened. "Oh, is that all? You birds don't have too many legends, but the ones you do have are real humdingers."

Well, it was only a dream, so there's no need to worry.

But Arnie was very worried indeed.

The next day, Bobby, Kat and Teabag were sat in their English class waiting for their teacher to arrive.

Kat was flicking Teabag's ears. "What's the matter with you, Teabag? You haven't said a word all morning."

"I was thinking about my Curly Wurlys. I hope whoever finds them loves them as much as me."

"You certainly take your chocolate seriously," said Bobby.

"Chocolate's a very serious business."

Mr Buxton entered the classroom and slammed a pile of exercise books down on his desk. He lifted a number of books up and began throwing them towards the children. "Warris, very good." Whizz. "Carter, poor." Whizz. "Garrett, excellent." Whizz. He carried on distributing the

115

exercise books in this way, and the amazing thing was he didn't even look up as he was throwing them.

The children plucked the whizzing books out of the air and immediately opened them to see what mark they had got.

"Perkins." Whizz. "Now then Perkins, I see your essay was entitled Amnesia. For those of you who don't know, amnesia is a temporary loss of memory. Yet to my great surprise I find nothing written underneath. Did you write in invisible ink, Perkins?" There were several sniggers and a couple of guffaws from the children. The teacher continued his verbal assault. "Sit up straight, lad. Whatever possessed you to commit such an act of utter stupidity?"

"Er, okay, Sir," Perkins stuttered. "I was going to write my essay on amnesia, and then I had a temporary loss of memory." Perkins sat there with an idiotic grin plastered all over his face, as the rest of the class laughed behind their hands as quietly as they could.

Mr Buxton glared at Perkins and the boy began to blush so fiercely that the children sitting nearby could feel the waves of heat from his face. After an eternity of glaring the teacher began to speak in a slow measured way. "In all the years I've been teaching I never believed I would come across a boy with the brains of a wombat." More laughter from the children. The teacher rubbed his forehead as if he was getting a headache before continuing to speak. "Let's hope you don't forget about tonight's detention."

"Aw no, Sir," cried Perkins, "it's the end of term."

"You should have *remembered* that before you decided to try it on," said the teacher with a wide smile. "Perhaps next term you'll *remember* to treat me with a little more respect."

Perkins sat there, quietly fuming, as the teacher whizzed out the rest of the books.

When he reached the last book he looked up. "Carter, where are you? Stop hiding, lad. Did you write this, or did you let a squashed slug loose on the paper?"

"I wrote it, Sir," Carter answered, looking in the wrong direction.

Mr Buxton held up three fingers. "How many fingers am I holding up?"

Someone pointed Carter in the right direction.

"Sixteen?"

More laughter.

"Sixteen!" cried the teacher. "That's an impossibility. I think you'd better see an optician in the holidays because you might just be needing glasses."

"Yes, Sir," said Carter, staring at the hat stand in the corner.

"Right then," began the teacher, "as it's the last day of term I thought I'd give you a nice easy lesson. Using as many of the words from this weeks spelling test as you can, I would like an essay on heroes and villains. You can write about someone famous, or someone you know, or even a fictional character, as long as they are a hero or a villain. And I don't want anyone writing about me."

Perkins tutted.

"Okay then," continued Mr Buxton, "get writing. And do it in silence. Carter put that banana down. Your pen's fallen on the floor, lad."

Carter fell out of his chair and searched for his pen, until his best friend picked it up and guided the boy back to his seat.

While they were writing, Teabag noticed that Bobby had a piece of paper sticking out of his back pocket. He pulled out the paper. Written at the top of the old parchment it said, The Banishment Spell. Teabag did what everybody else in his shoes would have done and read out the spell.

And Perkins disappeared.

"Whoops," said Teabag.

Then the paper in Teabag's hand began glowing blue and burst into golden flames. Teabag dropped the burning paper and stamped it out amongst a spray of orange sparks. (The banishment spell had been designed to self-destruct after it had been used six times.)

Mr Buxton sat up. "Who's messing with fire?"

Teabag finished dancing up and down on the smoking parchment. "Sir, my essay just burst into flames."

"If you are playing with matchsticks, laddie, you'll spend the rest of your life writing lines."

Teabag grimaced. "It must have been a kind of spontaneous combustion thing, Sir. It happens every now and again."

Bobby glanced over his shoulder. "Your essay's still on your desk."

"Er, I've got a confession to make," admitted Teabag, "and you're going to be a teensy weensy bit annoyed with me."

Mr Buxton decided to give Teabag the benefit of the doubt, as he was normally very well behaved, and because it was the end of term and he was in a very good mood. The teacher was suddenly startled out of his daydreams, by the voice of Bobby Coleman shouting. "You did what?!!"

That was the last straw, and as a punishment, he set Bobby and Teabag a different essay and told them to finish it off as homework.

The two boys sat there scratching their heads and wondering what to write.

Mr Buxton lounged in his chair with a sadistic grin on his face, because the essay he had given them was, One Hundred Things I Know About the Inside of a Ping Pong Ball.

The only sound in the classroom was that of the two boys rattling their brains.

Mr Buxton relaxed in his chair. Everything was perfect. And then he noticed that Perkins was missing.

On the way home, Bobby was chastising Teabag about reading the magic spell.

"How was I supposed to know that it was a demonic incantation?" said Teabag in self-defence.

"You shouldn't have took it in the first place," growled Bobby.

Teabag cringed. "I think it made Perkins disappear."

"Oh, that's marvellous!" cried Bobby.

They walked home in silence as Bobby was too mad to speak, and Teabag was too scared to.

After Bobby had calmed down a smidge he glanced at Teabag. "How many things did you know about the inside of the ping pong ball?"

"I could only think of three."

"That many?"

CHAPTER SEVENTEEN

CONFLICT

Bobby decided to take some flowers to Thelma's grave in Witches Woods, because, well, because it was a nice thing to do. He was going to take some forget-me-nots, but Thelma would have considered this a bit soppy, and so he took a bunch of wolf's bane instead. He kneeled by the grave and laid the flowers down and told the ex-witch about some of the adventures he'd been on, and all the Superpowers the green flames had given him. As he talked, a pair of violet eyes observed him from underneath a dark hood.

In the silence of the woods, he had time to reflect on all that had happened to him over the last few months. He wondered if he would ever have an ordinary life like everybody else. It was getting close to Christmas and a tiny robin landed on a nearby log.

The robin seemed to be staring straight at Bobby which made him feel a little uneasy.

I wonder what that great lump is doing in Witches Woods at this time of night?

"I am not a great lump," said Bobby.

You can read my thoughts, can you? You must be Arnie's pet.

"I think you'll find that Arnie is my pet."

Whatever. He's a nice budgie, you know. He, and Attila the crow, are my best friends around here.

"Do you mind if I ask you a question?"

Fire away, human.

"Why do we only see robins at Christmas?"

Because the rest of the year we go surfing in Bermuda, that's where we get our red chests. It's a touch of sun burn.

"Why do all you birds treat me as if I'm stupid?"

Maybe we know something you don't. I'm off now, because I also know it's better not to be in Witches Woods after dark. Bye bye.

The robin flew off.

Bobby certainly regarded birds in a different light now he could read their thoughts, because he never would have believed that they were so sharp. He was sat there wondering why he could only read the thoughts of birds, and as he was thinking this, a dark creature floated out from behind the trees and landed before him. Bobby lifted his head and he felt a million cold fingers crawling up and down his spine as he recognised the shadowy creature from last night's dream.

The Figure's deep violet eyes shone bright. "I was wondering if you could point the way to the rest of the world, because I have an appointment with it in a short while." Ice dripped from its every word.

The youngster found his voice and cautiously said. "I've seen you in my dreams."

"Would that be the one where I rip your friends' hearts out and throw you to your death." The Figure glared steadily into the youngster's eyes. "Don't look so surprised, I put that dream inside your head."

"I know who you are."

"And how do you know that?"

"A little bird told me."

"Then you know that I signal the end of the world," hissed the Figure

"I've fought evil people before, you know," Bobby

121

said defiantly.

"Yes, I know, and well done for that," mocked the Figure. "But even though they were evil, they had no imagination. I have, and an evil imagination is *very* dangerous indeed."

Bobby regarded the Figure with curious eyes. "Why must you destroy the earth?"

The Figure simply said. "It is fate."

Bobby sprang to his feet and snarled. "I don't believe in fate."

Then something incredible happened. The colours in the woods began to swirl and tumble and whirl until they were nothing but a blur. When the colours had ceased spinning and rearranged themselves they were standing in the top room of the old railway station.

"So you don't believe in fate, Coleman," taunted the Figure. "Can you remember your dream from last night?" The figure stared at the nodding boy. "Good, then you will be pleased to know that your two friends are on their way here right now. Do you believe in fate now?"

Last night's dream was actually coming true and our Superhero suddenly felt very powerless indeed. He noticed the iron poker next to the blazing fire and he picked it up and threw it as hard as he could. The poker cut through the air like an arrow and pierced through the chest of the Figure. Bulls-eye!

But the Figure did not collapse to the ground. It casually curled its long thin fingers around the poker and slowly pulled it out.

"That's not possible," cried Bobby. "It went straight through your heart."

The Figure glared at him with those evil violet eyes. "I haven't got a heart."

Bobby felt as though all the blood had been drained

from his face as he realised that there was nothing he could do.

Then he remembered his ruby lighter, and he whipped it out of his pocket, lit the flame, and blew a raging fire right at the Figure.

The fire engulfed the Figure, but after the flames had died out, it stood there totally unscathed. The Figure laughed. "There is no escaping fate, my friend, as I am sure you will find out when your friends arrive." It opened out its hands revealing long slender fingers, and on the tips of each finger there were eight shiny silver blades. It placed one under Bobby's chin and hissed. "I will give them a *heart felt* welcome."

Although Bobby knew it was futile he punched the Figure right in the face as hard as he could.

This caught the diabolical creature by surprise and it yelped in pain.

Bobby crowed triumphantly. "I see the mighty Figure can be hurt."

The Figure grabbed him by the throat and lifted him into the air. It spat these words right into his face. "I am going to make you pay for that, you worm. I've decided on a change of plan, you maggot. I'm not going to throw you to your death. I'm going to rip your heart out instead, and then I can watch your face as you die."

At that moment Arnie swooped through the window.

Put him down you great big wazzock.

The Figure, not being able to read the budgie's thoughts, kept a tight grip on Bobby's throat.

Arnie flew straight under the Figure's hood and furiously pecked at its face until it dropped Bobby and swept him away with its arms.

The Figure held them steady in its gaze and spoke in a cool whisper. "The more you resist me, the more painful I will make your deaths." It raised its hand to strike at

Bobby's heart.

Bobby couldn't understand why time hadn't stopped, as it usually did when he was afraid, because right now he was more than terrified. It seems as if the Figure was right. There's no escaping fate. As he watched the light glinting off the tiny blades on the Figure's hands, he prepared himself to die. It was then the miracle happened.

There was a flash of bright green light from the other side of the room, and something quite strange was happening to Arnie. A transparent cocoon enveloped the small bird and in this cocoon there was a dance of green light taking place. Every shade of green under the sun danced and circled inside, until the light gradually faded away, and the cocoon was now swirling with smoke. Then a tiny crack appeared on the surface of the cocoon and this crack began to spread out until the cocoon was split into two.

As the smoke drifted away an old man emerged. He was completely bald and he was wearing a pair of glasses with copper tinted lenses, and a flame red suit with smoke grey shoes. Amazingly enough, Arnie had transformed into this old man.

"Who the hell are you?" snarled the Figure.

The old man smiled. "Don't you recognise me?"

The Figure seemed puzzled for a moment. "Pappa Rapper Stone? A few years older, but it *is* you. Will you *never* die?"

"Not while we have unfinished business."

"You can die today then," taunted the Figure, "with the rest of this sorry looking planet."

The Figure and Pappa Rapper Stone grasped each other by the throat and began a titanic fight to the death. Fire and Brimstone poured from their eyes. Sand and Starlight dripped from their brows. Hydrogen and Helium hissed out of their mouths. The North, West, East and South winds blew through the windows and raged around the room. And all these special elements drew the heat from the fire until the raging storm burnt a chasm open in the Universe.

Through this chasm Bobby witnessed a darkness that was blacker than black, which reached towards infinity.

As the mortal enemies edged closer to the abyss, Pappa rasped through gritted teeth. "If I fall into the darkness, I'll take you with me."

"You *will* be lost in the shadows of infinity," the Figure whispered with relish, "but *I* will stay to see the Earth has no tomorrow."

Pappa lost his balance and teetered on the edge of the chasm, and then he lost his footing and slipped into the abyss, but he caught hold of the Figure's arm and dragged it down with him.

Bobby shook himself from the trance he was in and ran to the edge of the abyss thrusting his hand in and catching hold of Pappa's arm. Bobby's arm became frozen in the darkness of the universe, but he pulled with all his might and seconds later Pappa was able to reach inside the room and haul himself out.

The Figure was holding on to his leg, and he looked up at Pappa and whimpered. "Please, Pappa Rapper Stone, save me. You are a good man, show me some mercy."

Pappa swivelled round and sat on the edge of the abyss and kicked the Figure square in the chest. "I'll show you as much mercy as all the millions of innocent people you have murdered on all the planets you have destroyed!" He slammed his foot down again.

The Figure screamed through the raging dark winds. "It was their fate, you fool! It was their time to die!"

"And *now* it is yours!" cried the tiny old man as he

smashed his foot down with all the force of a giant and condemned the screaming Figure to oblivion.

The old man and the young Superhero watched in silence as the Figure fell kicking and screaming deeper and deeper into the darkness until he could be seen no more.

Pappa Rapper Stone whispered. "The world can rest in peace. The Figure is no more."

The dark storm winds dropped and the chasm slowly closed.

Bobby was in a state of shock and all he could say was. "Didn't you use to be my budgie?"

"Take my hand," said Pappa Rapper Stone.

Bobby was too dumbfounded to ask why, so he took the old man's hand and they flew out of the window and soared over the houses of Milltown.

As soon as they had flown out of the window, Kat and Teabag burst through the door and quickly scanned the room.

Teabag swung round to Kat. "I could have sworn I heard voices."

"It must have been the mad ghost of the old station master."

Teabag giggled nervously. "Don't be daft."

"Who else could it have been?"

"Arrgh!!" screamed Teabag as he sprinted down the stairs.

"Arrgh!!" screamed Kat as she sprinted down after him.

CHAPTER EIGHTEEN

THE FELLOWSHIP AND BEYOND

Pappa Rapper Stone was soaring above the clouds.

Bobby held on tightly. "Where are we going?"

"We are heading for the hole in the ozone layer. Once we are through we arrive at the Chamber in the Sky, and that is where all your fellow Superheroes gather for their monthly meeting."

"You're not Arnie the budgie, then?"

"Thelma told me that you had fallen in the magic flames," replied Pappa Rapper Stone, "and so we knew you would gain Superpowers. I always like to spend a few months with a new recruit and being a budgie was the perfect way to observe you. Now you are ready to strike out on your own."

"Who *are* you then?"

"I was born so long ago that I forget my real name," the old man began. "I was born and bred in London, and I moved to Liverpool when I was ten. I gained my Superpowers when I was a young teenage fisherman, and I saved a mermaid from a trawler's net. She sang me a beautiful dolphin's song, then touched my hair and said I was blessed. Now I am Pappa Rapper Stone, the most elderly Superhero in England, and I am the Head of the Fellowship."

"You're the boss then?"

"I suppose I am."

It wasn't long before they arrived at the Chamber in

the Sky, and Pappa led Bobby through a large oak door into a wonderfully old fashioned room that belonged in an old castle, like Camelot.

As Bobby stood there taking in the view, a slight girl approached him and shook his hand. "My name is Fireball and I'm very pleased to meet you."

"Are you a Superhero?" asked Bobby.

"I suppose I am," answered Fireball.

"But *you're* not American."

"I know I'm not, I'm from Rotherham."

"I've never heard of a Superhero called Fireball."

"Only my Superfriends get to call me that."

"I'm not your friend."

"You soon will be, Milltown boy."

There was a large wooden oval table in the centre of the room and around this table there were fourteen girls and boys aged from ten to fifteen.

Pappa Rapper Stone rapped on the table a few times to get everybody's attention. "This is Bobby Coleman, and he is the fifteenth member of our Society."

"What Society is that?" asked Bobby.

"We are the English Fellowship of Young Superheroes. You are our latest recruit. Introduce yourselves, children."

The children called out their names, one by one:

"Silver Catfish."

"Mega Boy."

"Lady Viper."

"Black Laser."

"Aurora."

"Iron Fist."

"Micro Boy."

"Wasp Girl."

"Dragon Eyes."

"King Raven."
"Machine Boy."
"Ant Girl."
"Ice Girl."
"Fireball."

Bobby said hello to them all. "I haven't heard of a single one of you."

"This is the way we want it to be," said Pappa Rapper Stone. "We don't want fame like all the American Superheroes as it gets in the way of our work. These children have saved the world from all kinds of disasters, and the only glamour they allow themselves are their Superhero names. Though we are the only ones who use these names. Now, Bobby Coleman, it is time for you to choose your name."

"I don't know what to call myself."

"Think about it while we eat our meal," suggested Fireball.

Bobby glanced at his watch. "I have to get home, it's getting late."

"There's no rush," said Fireball. "Time never passes while we're in this room."

So Bobby sat down and tucked into his meal while he talked to some of the other Superheroes.

Black Laser told him how she had burnt her way through the ground earlier that evening to save a young boy who had been buried in a cavern underground. She said the boy's name was Toby Perkins and he had no recollection of how he got underground.

Bobby didn't mention the Banishment Spell, or that Perkins was his classmate at school.

After the meal, Bobby stood up and announced. "As I received my Superpowers from a magic *green* flame, I'd like to be called, Emerald."

"A fine name," said Pappa Rapper Stone. "Welcome to the Fellowship."

Before Bobby was taken home, Pappa told him to carry on as normal. He told him that if his Superpowers weren't enough to kill a certain foe, the Fellowship would send help, and by co-operating in this way, the planet would always be safe.

As they were flying back to Milltown, Bobby said. "Will I have to fight villains for the rest of my life?"

"That is entirely up to you," Pappa replied, "as you can retire whenever you want. Most of the Fellowship's Superheroes retire when they stop enjoying the fight, and that's probably the best way of doing it." Pappa Rapper Stone landed in Bobby's garden. "I will come back a month from today to take you to our next meeting. Until then, Emerald, goodbye and good luck."

Pappa Rapper Stone took off and left him alone in the moonlight.

It felt good being called Emerald.

But Bobby was absolutely exhausted and would sleep very well tonight.

The next day Bobby woke up to a bright sunny Saturday morning. He put on his jeans and a sweatshirt and went downstairs. His dad was slumped in the armchair watching the news and his mum was cooking egg and bacon for breakfast.

Anna smiled at her brother. "Follow me."

He followed her into the back garden.

Anna pointed to a tiny robin redbreast perched on a pitch fork next to the shed. "I think she's tame. Can we keep her?"

"How do you know it's a girl?"

"I just know."

"Well, she can stay with us if she wants to."

"Thank you, Bobby. I think she wants to." And Anna skipped back to the house.

Hello again.

The robin saluted Bobby with her left wing.

Your sister was right. I am a girl and my name is Rosabella.

"Rosabella the robin. I won't have any trouble remembering that. I think it's only fair to tell you that Arnie's gone, as I know he was a good friend of yours."

I know. He told me everything, and, if you don't mind, I would like to tag along on some of your adventures, you may even find I can help you.

"Don't you have to go surfing in Bermuda after Christmas?"

You shouldn't believe everything you're told.

Rosabella looked over to the house.

If I'm going to be moving in with the Coleman family, I better get one or two things from my nest.

Later that day, Kat and Teabag called, and told Bobby they'd heard the mad ghost of the station master again.

Teabag rubbed his hands together. "Maybe we should hold a séance and find out why he's so mad and restless."

"I'll tell you why he's so mad and restless," said Kat. "Half the kids in the neighbourhood go running round his station."

"Maybe we should stop going there," suggested Bobby.

"I think you're right," agreed Teabag. "Now that we're all teenagers, I think we should start acting more like grown-ups."

The children looked at each other for a couple of seconds and then they all collapsed with laughter, because acting like grown-ups is strictly for the grown-ups. Then the children discussed the more serious things in life, like which would be the fastest down the cycle path, a tea tray or a skateboard.

Bobby would stay friends with Kat and Teabag throughout the rest of his life, but they never ever found out he was a Superhero.

A couple of weeks later, Bobby was lying on his bed watching a new game show called, How Tall is My Dog? He was wondering who thought up these shows and whether they were in possession of a brain, when Rosabella flew in through the window.

You're not going to believe this.

"If the world needs saving then let the American Superheroes do it, I'm watching the telly."

That's not a very good attitude for a Superhero.

"Why don't you look under S in the yellow pages. Then you can give one of the other Superheroes a call?"

I don't think Pappa Rapper Stone would want to hear you talking like this.

"Okay, I'm coming," said Bobby moving as slowly as he could. "Look at me getting up, look at me getting my blue moonstone and my ruby lighter, look at me... "

Alright, alright, I get the picture. Hey, is that How Tall is My Dog? Ah flip, I always seem to miss my favourite programmes.

When they were outside, Rosabella fluttered down and landed on Bobby's shoulder.

Bobby turned to the little bird. "What does Rosabella stand for? It wouldn't be annoying little robin, would it?"

Rosabella ruffled up her feathers.

No wonder Arnie changed into somebody else.

"I'm only kidding," said Bobby. "I think Rosabella is a lovely name."

Come on now, Bobby, we don't want a soft, soppy

ending, do we?

"I suppose you're right," said Bobby. "What's the emergency this time, then?"

Well, when I was flying around earlier on, I noticed a flock of mutant pterodactyls heading this way, and I think they intend eating their way through the whole town.

"Mutant pterodactyls?"

That's correct.

"This looks like a job for Emerald."

And so, Emerald and the tiny robin redbreast walked into the sunset in search of the mutant pterodactyls.